Advance Praise for
I Never Said That I Was Brave

"In Tasneem Jamal's quietly compelling novel, a tragic discovery is the catalyst for the unnamed narrator to tell the story of her complicated relationship with the seductive, selfish, magnetic force that is her friend Miriam. This story is woven through with threads of memory, and the mysterious, invisible forces that hold people together or pull them apart. With a special sensitivity for entanglements of the heart, *I Never Said That I Was Brave* explores the devastating consequences when those who know us the best, hurt us the worst."
—Anuja Varghese, author of the Governor General's Literary Award–winning *Chrysalis*

"In Tasneem Jamal's beautifully written, remarkably intimate novel, the shadow side of enduring friendship is inextricably entangled with its sweetness—evoking a sense of awe for the lengths to which a person will go to be loved, and to love." —Carrie Snyder, author of *Girl Runner* and *Francie's Got a Gun*

"This is a beautiful, hypnotic, and searching novel told with the intimacy and honesty one might find in a cherished friend." —Camilla Gibb, author of *The Relatives*

T0243306

"*I Never Said That I Was Brave* pulled me in from the first line. An unnamed narrator speaks directly to the reader as she reconstructs her relationship with her closest friend, one of rivalry, tragedy, and fierce devotion. She rebuilds, recalls, falters, revises, re-orders, and loops through time and the slippery nature of her thoughts and timelines adds a rich layer to this compelling and devastating story of friendship. In masterful prose, Tasneem Jamal shows us the intricacies of memory and how we shape it to tell the stories of our lives. I never stopped asking, what next? After reading the final line, I started again from the beginning. I loved this book, and you will too." —Emily Urquhart, author of *Ordinary Wonder Tales*

I Never Said That I Was Brave

I Never Said That I Was Brave

a novel

Tasneem Jamal

ANANSI

Published in Canada in 2024 and the USA in 2024 by House of Anansi Press Inc.
houseofanansi.com

House of Anansi Press is committed to protecting our natural environment.
This book is made of material from well-managed FSC®-certified forests, recycled
materials, and other controlled sources.

House of Anansi Press is a Global Certified Accessible™ (GCA by Benetech)
publisher. The ebook version of this book meets stringent accessibility standards
and is available to readers with print disabilities.

28 27 26 25 24   1 2 3 4 5

Library and Archives Canada Cataloguing in Publication

Title: I never said that I was brave : a novel / Tasneem Jamal.
Names: Jamal, Tasneem, author.
Identifiers: Canadiana (print) 20240353692 | Canadiana (ebook) 20240353706 |
ISBN 9781487012823 (softcover) | ISBN 9781487012830 (EPUB)
Subjects: LCGFT: Novels.
Classification: LCC PS8619.A44 I5 2024 | DDC C813/.6—dc23

Cover design: Sharon Kish
Cover image: iStock.com/Dusan Stankovic

*House of Anansi Press is grateful for the privilege to work on and create from the
Traditional Territory of many Nations, including the Anishinabeg, the Wendat, and the
Haudenosaunee, as well as the Treaty Lands of the Mississaugas of the Credit.*

With the participation of the Government of Canada
Avec la participation du gouvernement du Canada | Canadä

*We acknowledge for their financial support of our publishing program the Canada
Council for the Arts, the Ontario Arts Council, and the Government of Canada.*

Printed and bound in Canada

This book is printed on FSC® certified paper.

To Mia and Lily,
who used to dwell among the stars—
and were summoned to the earth for me

Prologue

I SHOULD TELL YOU straight away that Miriam and I had been out of touch for almost two years before she died. No phone calls, no letters, no emails. Nothing. She didn't want to speak to me, and I respected this. I would go so far as to say I understood it. I carried on with my life and she carried on with hers (as far as I know). It was a particularly busy time for me in those days, what with a new house and a change in job. My life was moving forward rapidly.

Then Miriam died and the undercurrent of my existence shifted. Certainly, I continued to do what I had done before, to wake up and go to work, to make dinners and water the plants, but I felt, if not stalled, slowed down, as you are, for example, in the moment before you change direction. The new coat of paint I had wanted so keenly to add to my living room walls no longer seemed important. My colleagues, undoubtedly frustrated by my repeatedly turning down lunch requests, stopped inviting me to any social events altogether. At night, I had terrifying dreams, usually some manner of the following: I am inexplicably on a ladder or a mountain or a balcony high in the sky in some nebulous place, so overcome by the fear of falling that I cannot move; I am walking in a park in the city and encounter a bear (or a lion or a tiger), enormous and terrifying. I always woke up before I fell, before I was devoured, but with adrenalin coursing through my veins. And, so, I would lie in bed staring at the darkened ceiling, desperate but unable to sleep. All too soon, images of Miriam would come, unbidden. Miriam when we were children. Miriam when we were at university. Miriam during those final, terrible years.

During the day, I would feel her presence in small, strange ways. For example, sometimes when I was driving my car, I would catch myself holding the steering wheel as she used to, with her left hand only, her right hand limp by her side, habitually freed to shift gears after years of driving a manual transmission. Once in the springtime I sat on the back deck and blinked slowly as I stared at a warbler jumping from branch to branch on the largest maple tree in my yard, and it was Miriam who was blinking; it was Miriam who was living this moment in my life. Initially, these experiences were startling, but I grew accustomed to them. They weren't unpleasant so much as disconcerting. It's difficult to convey how these episodes left me feeling except to say that during and immediately afterwards I was overwhelmed by a sense that Miriam was present, not as a ghost upon whom I laid my eyes but as a presence indistinct from my own.

At the time of her death, Miriam had been staying in a small house in the BC Interior. I don't know if she owned this house or if she was renting it or how, for that matter, she was paying for it at all. I don't know how long she had been living there. I know only the following facts. One November day, probably early in the morning but no one has pinpointed exactly when, Miriam started her car, a Honda Civic manufactured in the 1980s and not equipped with a catalytic converter. This detail is important because of what happened next. Miriam let the car's ignition run with the garage door closed and the car's windows open. A day or two later (it is not clear, as I say, when exactly she started the engine) she was found dead in the back seat of the Civic. Miriam's four-year-old daughter, Zara, wrapped in a flannel blanket and her mother's arms, was also dead.

MIRIAM'S WORK OR—as she described it to me many times—her "calling" was to understand the darkness in the universe. I mean this literally. Miriam was an astrophysicist and her research focused on dark matter. The visible universe is only a fraction of what scientists such as Miriam know exists. The majority of the universe is invisible, mysterious. And this mystery is what stirred Miriam, what excited her as nothing else in her life could do. I can see her now, her dyed brown hair pulled into a messy bun, her slender frame covered by a bulky black turtleneck on a cold winter night—a choice much too heavy, as it turns out, for this steamy Indian restaurant on Bloor Street, her favourite, not mine.

I can hear her.

Dark matter holds the universe together. It's what keeps everything from coming apart. Do you understand? But she doesn't pause for me to respond, to remind her she has told me this before, many, many times. *We know dark matter exists because it distorts what we can see. The more dark matter there is, the greater the distortion. So, it's like this: We can't perceive dark matter because it doesn't interact with light. But it does interact with gravity. Therefore, we can prove dark matter exists because we can see its effect. The distortion in the visible reveals the unknown.*

Do you get it?

She is leaning towards me, beads of sweat on her upper lip, the makeup she had on earlier now absorbed by her skin so that her face is ghostly pale. *Do you understand?*

This is what Miriam does to me. Always. She demands my attention. But I don't understand. There is so much I don't understand. I am speaking now of things beyond gravitational forces and cosmology. And here we have arrived at my motivation for telling you about Miriam and about everything that happened, from the beginning. You see, if I try to make you understand, perhaps I will understand—not only Miriam's choices, but also mine.

Part I

Entanglement

Chapter 1

MIRIAM USED TO say that the years living on Banting Place were the happiest of her life. She lived in that low-cost townhouse complex in Kitchener from the age of eight or nine until she turned twelve. I've no doubt she was happy then; indeed, I witnessed some of this happiness. And though childhood is a long time ago, I too can remember the joys of being a preteen, the magical time of no responsibilities or cares, when you haven't yet begun to wonder whether you are smart or pretty or neither. But to describe it as the happiest period of an entire lifetime would be akin to saying your happiest years were when you were a toddler. Or an infant.

And, so, whenever Miriam would evoke the joys of Banting Place I would smile politely while inwardly dismissing her words as a bit, well, childish. The truth is, I don't know why it bothered me so much, Miriam's insistence that three or four joyous years from her girlhood were never surpassed or even matched in the ensuing decades of her life. It occurs to me only now how sad this declaration is.

Many years before Miriam began to distinguish her life in terms of happy and thus not-happy years, my father facilitated the sale of the Banting Place townhouse. About three months earlier, when Miriam was twelve, her mother, Begum, had decided to move to Burnaby. But before moving, she leased her townhouse to a group of young men. Within only a few months, Begum became unexpectedly (unexpectedly to us, anyways) engaged to be married. Her fiancé wanted to buy a new house for the family in British Columbia, using in part the proceeds from the sale of the Banting Place property. My father agreed to look after the transaction because Begum was family, albeit distant family. She was my father's second cousin, once removed. We don't use such descriptors in my family. In Gujarati my father would describe Begum as "apra gamvari," which means literally "someone from our village." But he couldn't accurately translate this into English because none of us is actually from a village and we really are related. So, when he talked about her to the white real estate agent, he referred to her as his "niece." The first time he did this my mother widened her eyes and explained to the bemused agent that Begum was in fact my father's middle-aged contemporary and not some "young girl."

When Begum telephoned the renters and informed them that her house was being put on the market and that they would have to move out, they became angry and refused. After some litigation they had no choice. The day they were to have vacated it, my father arrived at the Banting Place townhouse and found that the young men had indeed left. But they had taken a sledgehammer to the house. They smashed through drywall and destroyed closet doors. They spray painted walls, ripped out appliances, and poured cooking oil on the carpets. All attempts to locate the vengeful renters failed. Begum was left to absorb the cost of the repairs from the eventual sale of the house. She must have been crushed, but I know nothing of her reaction; I don't remember my father even mentioning it. I remember only what he said about the townhouse, that despite the substantial damage on the inside, the outside looked perfect. The renters had not touched the windows or the front door. When my father described what had become of Miriam's former home, I pictured a woman whose abusive husband chooses words rather than fists to beat her.

But before the Banting Place townhouse was smashed by angry renters, before Miriam and her mother moved to Burnaby, from the time I was nine and she was ten until I was eleven and she was twelve and living in the midst of her happiest years, Miriam and I forged a bond that would last the rest of our lives, enduring even my betrayal and her death.

MIRIAM AND I had known each other since birth, my birth, to be precise, which came sixteen months after hers. Our parents were connected not only by blood but also by friendship. In fact, it was my mother who gave Miriam her name. "I was in Mbarara Hospital because of my own pregnancy," my mother told Miriam as I looked on, having heard this story in the context of my brother's birth, which came mere days after Miriam's. "I held you before even your father had seen you and I said, 'Oh, Maryam!' I don't know why I said it. The name just came out of my mouth. Your parents liked it. But your father spelled it differently and told people that he chose your name."

Not long after Miriam heard this story, while she and I were in the Kitchener Public Library (it was walking distance from Banting Place and I loved libraries, even then), we decided on a whim to look up the meaning of our names. As it was the late 1970s, my name did not exist in any books we could find but hers was there.

"Miriam," she read aloud, "Hebrew: from the root words for bitter and rebellion."

"What does that mean?" I asked her.

"It means my name comes from two Hebrew words. Bitter means, you know, angry and grumpy. Disappointed by everything. Rebellion is when you fight to be free. Luke Skywalker is a rebel fighter. The Rebellion is fighting the Galactic Empire. Like that."

"Rebels are the good guys," I said, "who fight because they are bitter?" I was thoroughly confused.

But Miriam was reading again and ignored me. "Miriam, a form of Mary, was also the name of the mother of Jesus."

That evening I asked my mother, in a somewhat accusatory tone, why she gave Miriam a Christian name.

"Jesus is a prophet in the Quran," my mother said in strangely formal English and then switched to her customary Punjabi. "Actually, at that time I didn't know about Jesus's mother. I once had a dear friend in school named Maryam, and she had the same dimple in her chin as I saw in Begum's baby." My mother paused and her face became bright, as though a lightbulb somewhere inside her had come on. "I hadn't thought of my friend for years. Then I saw this baby and for one strange moment I thought I was looking at her, born again."

My mother had never mentioned a classmate before; indeed, she had never mentioned her school days before. "Did your friend die?" I asked.

She looked at me, startled. "No, no. That's not what I meant. When I said she was born again I meant she had come back into my life. But that's silly, isn't it?" My mother was smiling when she said this but the light in her face had gone out. "Maryam left school when we were in primary. I don't know where she is now. But she must have become a wife and a mother like me. Like every other girl."

It would be a long time before I gave much thought to the meaning of Miriam's name, or my own. But for the next few years, when my teachers showed us story-books about the birth of Jesus, in my mind I saw on the placid, unsmiling face of Mary a quiet anger and an unspoken disappointment.

It occurs to me this is a good time to tell you some-thing I am just now recalling. It was an evening in 1994 and my mother had telephoned to tell me she received Miriam's wedding invitation in the mail. Miriam had been calling herself Mary—informally—for a few years, but my mother and I were startled to see it embossed on a card announcing something as important as her wedding.

"Why did she change her name?" my mother asked.

"She didn't change it. She anglicized it." I said this with an impatience that surprised me considering I too was dismayed by the card. In fact, a few years earlier when Miriam told me about her intention to start call-ing herself Mary, I had not been supportive. We were standing outside a restaurant on Granville Street in Vancouver. I can't recall if we had just come out of the restaurant or were about to enter, but I know it was 1991. She was living in Vancouver then, doing her under-graduate degree, and I had visited her that spring.

"What's wrong with your name?" I asked. "It's a great name. It's easy for English speakers to pronounce,

ˌisn't it? It's Hebrew and Arabic. It's ancient. But more importantly, it's who you are, Miriam. Honestly, would you throw all that away? For what? Do you want to be white that badly?" I didn't say all this in one breath. I paused after each question, waiting for her to answer. She might have nodded or said a word here and there in response. I can't recall precisely how the conversation went, but I wasn't as judgmental as I might sound in this recounting. The point is I was shocked.

What I do remember clearly is that when my questions had been exhausted, she shrugged. And then she fixed her eyes on mine. Until then she had been looking around, not in any unusual way, simply taking in her surroundings as we all tend to do, turning at the sound of a car horn or a loud voice. Sometimes she glanced at me or behind me. But now her gaze was locked on me. It's difficult to describe the expression on her face in that moment; it was as though she wanted to convey something without using words because she could never take the words back.

You aren't worthy of an explanation.

She didn't say this to me, not then, not ever. But I believed this is what she meant with that look.

I'm getting ahead of myself. I had intended only to tell you about Miriam's wedding invitation signalling a formal shift in how she addressed herself. Let me get back to describing the early days of our relationship.

Though Miriam and I were in each other's lives from our beginnings, it took us time to become friends. In

my earliest memories Miriam appeared as a noisy and
often disruptive presence no matter where we were, at a
party at someone's house, at jamat khana, at a wedding.
She would be making adults double over with laughter,
riling up toddlers, always moving, moving, moving as
though she couldn't be held to a spot, as though she
were a whirl of energy and not a thing at all. Miriam
didn't become a fully realized person for me until I was
nine and she was ten. I remember the moment clearly.
It was the night of the fight.

Heavyweight boxing champion Muhammad Ali was
a hero in my family. Boxing, or to be more accurate,
watching big championship bouts on television, was a
popular thing to do in those days. Ali was not only the
world champion, he was funny and smart and charm-
ing. And he was a Muslim. Muslims were almost never
on our televisions or movie screens, not even in Hindi
films in which all the heroes (and actors who played
them) were Hindu or purported to be. Ali was proud of
being a Muslim. As a result, my family talked about him
as though he were a distant relative of ours. And, so,
this is how I came to think of him. Remarkably, I felt the
same way about Rocky Balboa, who was not Muslim
or brown or "one of us" in any way. But I had watched
him struggle to get into shape and I had watched him
in his crummy apartment and I had watched him try
to be a good guy.

Only a few months earlier I had asked my brother,
Saif, a question that had been causing me no small

amount of distress. "Who is better, Muhammed Ali or Rocky?" I simply couldn't figure it out. They were both heavyweights, which meant they would vie for the same title. Whom did I want to win? I was pretty worked up about this.

Saif squinted at me while simultaneously shaking his head. "Rocky isn't real. That was a made-up movie." Even in those days it was obvious to me that Saif wasn't secure in his intelligence. When he had the opportunity to outsmart someone, even his little sister, he did so with relish. "Dummy," he added as he walked away.

I was stunned. Rocky was as real to me as Muhammed Ali. I suppose I could say I identified with both Ali and Rocky. But this doesn't quite capture the strength of the feeling. It seemed, as I watched either of them in a fight, as though I were Ali or Rocky. You should not infer from all this intensity of feeling about boxers that I was some sort of aficionado of the sport. I watched boxing matches because just about everyone—including boys and girls at school who were not Muslim—watched. But I didn't understand it in any meaningful way. What held my attention were the personal, even existential, stakes: Me versus the Other Guy; Me Fighting for My Life; Me Proving I'm Good Enough.

A few days after my ninth birthday, Muhammad Ali was in a fight to defend his world heavyweight title. The bout was on a school night but Saif and I were allowed to stay up to watch two or three rounds, which is all

we expected it would take for Ali to defeat the under-
dog with the gap-toothed smile. But round after round
Ali was not only unable to knock out Leon Spinks, he
sometimes would be on the ropes himself, getting
pummelled. My parents were so absorbed by the fight
they forgot to send us to bed. And, so, we watched until
the end, when the judges decided, without full agreement, that Leon Spinks had defeated Muhammad Ali.
"Someone was paid off," my father said, as my mother
finally ushered us off to bed. I fell asleep with a roiling
sensation in my chest and stomach, as though a calam-
ity had befallen my family. But there was a superficiality
to this feeling, so that by morning the overwhelming
sense of disaster was replaced by hunger, easily satiated
with a piece of toast and some Corn Flakes.

The Saturday after the Ali-Spinks fight we drove to
the nearby city of Guelph for a dinner party. Miriam
and her father and brother were at the party as well.
Miriam's parents had already been divorced for years
by then, so her mother wasn't with them. After dinner
or perhaps it was before, I can't recall this detail, all of
the children were playing in the unfinished basement
while the adults socialized upstairs. There were six of
us: Saif and me; Miriam and her brother, Salim; and
two other boys, both of whose names are not important to this telling. This basement was spacious and
poorly lit, and thus rife with imaginative possibilities
for children our age. It had two concrete support poles
in the middle of the room and exposed wooden studs

along the walls. There was no furniture or television or toys, but we seemed to have no trouble entertaining ourselves. Whenever we visited this house—and I recall we came here probably once every few months—I would race down to the basement, where I could run and jump and slide in my sock feet and not have to worry about breaking anything.

On this day the six of us children were discussing the Ali-Spinks fight. At one point Saif and Miriam took on the roles of Spinks and Ali respectively (there was a prior heated discussion about who would play whom, which was settled by a coin toss) and started a boxing match. They weren't actually throwing punches. They were hopping around each other, fists raised and held close by their own chins, in an effort to resolve our argument about who should have been awarded the fight's split decision. To my amazement, Saif and Salim insisted Spinks should indeed have been declared the winner. In the midst of our back and forth, which included my repeated insistence that someone had been paid off, increasingly loud shouting could be heard from upstairs. When the shouting reached a crescendo, we all froze. After a few moments, Miriam ran up the stairs and the rest of us followed. On the landing, I had to squeeze between Saif and Miriam to see what was happening. Across the room, I saw my father shouting words that for me became obscured by the sight of his arm outstretched, pointing across the room at a man who I know was a good friend of his, of someone holding him back as though if he were free to move, he would have lunged and attacked his friend like an animal. On the other side of the living room, the man was likewise being restrained and was likewise shouting. Between and around them other adults stood, hands over mouths or mouths agape, eyes fixed on one or the other man, cigarette smoke swirling in the air. The record playing on the turntable was stuck so that Lata Mangeshkar's sweet soprano kept repeating part of a line from a popular and mournful love song as though she were determined to be heard over the angry, shouting men: "Tera mera pyar amar" [Our love is eternal]—*scratch*—"Tera mera pyar amar"—*scratch*—"Tera mera pyar amar."

Miriam's father, Hassan Uncle, began shouting as well, first at my father then at the other man. He too was pointing, at one then the other, admonishing them not on the substance of their argument, whatever it was, but about their ridiculous behaviour. Hassan Uncle was using profane words, and I closed my eyes, terrified the argument was spreading like a fire. In the quiet of my mind, I silently completed the line of Lata's love song, one that I had heard countless times before on our own record player: *Tera mera pyar amar / Phir kyun mujhko lagta hai dar?* [Our love is eternal / Then why am I afraid?]

Hassan Uncle was laughing. Soon others joined him, including Miriam and Saif. I opened my eyes just as someone lifted the needle from the record and placed it past the scratch and into the middle of another song. The situation had been defused. My father and the other man were sitting down on a large ottoman, a broadly grinning Hassan Uncle between them. They were, if not happy, no longer insane. By the time we would leave, a few hours later, the two men were friends again.

Back in the basement an electric charge filled the air. I felt both ashamed and exhilarated by what I had witnessed and by the relief that it was over. The Ali-Spinks discussion was now replaced by the Upstairs Fight discussion. But because we were all in agreement that Hassan Uncle was the only respectable adult this evening, the conversation petered out quickly. The boys' talk turned to hockey, a sport in which I had little interest. I sat down and leaned against the wall, tired all of a sudden. Miriam, to my surprise, sat down beside me. She wasn't looking at me. She was staring at the boys. But when I followed her gaze, I saw that she was looking beyond them, into a darkened corner of the basement. She had never sat beside me like this, by choice.

"I saw *The Goodbye Girl* last week," I said. I didn't want her to leave and so I started speaking about a movie in the hopes this subject would hold her interest.

"Was it good?" she asked without turning to me.

I nodded. "It's about a woman who lives with her daughter in an apartment and this guy shows up and moves in and becomes the mom's boyfriend and the girl has a bike, like mine. With a banana seat. You know in movies how they have those old-fashioned bikes and never the banana seats and high handlebars? Well, this movie had a bike like we have." This particular detail in the movie thrilled me; it validated my world, and me. But I hadn't intended to go on so long about it. Miriam, still staring straight ahead, looked bored.

"*Close Encounters of the Third Kind* was good too," I said, trying again. "It's about UFOs—"

"I know," she said, cutting me off. "I saw it. Do you think they're real? Aliens? Guys with skinny, long arms and weird heads?"

"Yes," I said, without thinking, and then immediately regretted it. Miriam was looking at me now. I searched her face for signs that she thought I was a dummy. But I could detect none. "I guess I don't know if they have skinny arms or anything. But I feel like aliens are out there. I mean, why not? We're here."

She smiled.

We spent the rest of the evening talking about our favourite movies and television shows and racing around the basement pretending to be Steve Austin, the Six Million Dollar Man. We climbed onto a horizontal two-by-four beam, sat on our bums, and then pushed ourselves off, imagining we were leaping off a tall building. We did this again and again. At one point, something strange happened. It was minor and seemingly insignificant at the time, but the memory of it remains vivid in my mind. We were sitting atop the two-by-four beam ready to push off once more when Salim, Miriam's brother, walked past.

"Salim! Salim! Help!" Miriam called in a babyish voice of which I didn't think her capable. "Get me down! I'm stuck!" But she wasn't stuck. We'd jumped off this beam repeatedly and there was nothing on which to be stuck. Nor was it particularly high. Salim was thirteen, two and a half years older than Miriam, but he was considerably taller and bigger, almost as big as an adult. He reached up, put his hands under her arms and lifted his suddenly helpless sister down as though she were a toddler. He glanced in my direction, but I quickly jumped down for fear he would think I too wanted to be treated like a baby. He walked away and Miriam resumed our game, climbing up and leaping off, as though that odd interlude had never happened.

Chapter 2

S ALIM WAS A quiet boy, but he hadn't always been this way. The previous summer I had sat with him and about twenty other Ismaili children on a chartered school bus heading to London, Ontario, an hour's drive west of Kitchener, to visit a theme park called Storybook Gardens. I don't remember Miriam being with us. And though my brother was certainly somewhere near me on that bus, I don't recall seeing him either. Most of the families of the children on the trip had been in Canada for only a few years at that point and a group outing such as this—involving a charter travelling out of town—was unusual. Looking back, it occurs to me these children's outings were probably a failed experiment; after two or three similar trips, they stopped altogether. With respect to the London trip, I can recollect precisely nothing about Storybook Gardens itself, but I recall that the bus ride, particularly on the way back home, was a raucous affair. Small groups of children were talking over each other loudly or laughing uproariously. I don't think anything especially important or funny was being shared. We were all simply enjoying being together without any meaningful adult supervision (we did have a driver, a silver-haired white man, but he barely glanced at us, even when we boarded the bus). Out of the cacophony emerged the surprisingly powerful voice of one boy (Salim, I quickly ascertained). He was singing the words of a song that was popular at the time and almost immediately a few boys joined him in the chorus.

"Sing it!" shouted Salim. "Everybody!"

More children joined. Salim knew only a few lines of the song, which he kept repeating. But it didn't diminish our enjoyment. I joined others in slamming our feet on the floor of the bus and clapping to the rhythm.

Stomp, stomp. Clap. Stomp, stomp. Clap.

When Salim stood up in the aisle playing air guitar as the entire busload whooped and hollered, the driver pulled over. Standing up and facing us (and considerably shorter than I had imagined him to be), he shouted at us to sit down and shut up. Giggling, we did as he instructed, and the ride resumed, much quieter now though by no means silent.

I felt giddy. The experience had been glorious. And

25

Salim had been the star at the centre of it. He had been the sun.

Then he became eclipsed by a sullen and wholly uninteresting person. He even looked different. Salim had been an attractive little boy. His cheeks were plump and his features were well proportioned. But his face leaned out and black hair, too fine to be called a moustache but sufficiently thick and dark that it looked like a smudge of dirt, appeared on his upper lip; he walked with his shoulders hunched forward, as though a weight were pressing onto his upper back; and his voice became deeper, so that when he spoke, which more often than not involved only one-word utterances, he sounded like he was growling.

Though I spent a lot of time at Banting Place with Miriam, I rarely saw Salim. He preferred to spend his days alone in his bedroom. Music could often be heard coming from behind his closed door but sometimes there was only silence. On those occasions Miriam and I would stand outside his bedroom door, our ears pressed against the wood, trying to figure out what he could be doing. A few small stickers were plastered on that door: a Boston Bruins logo, a *No Smoking* sign, and a large purple-and-orange hippie flower. I liked the flower. It was cartoonish and reminded me of a teenage girl's bedroom, the kind I dreamed of having. Each time we were spying I would press an ear on the centre of the flower, as though this would somehow provide amplification. We never heard anything interesting, perhaps some shuffling or the dropping of an item; often we heard nothing at all. Salim was extraordinarily quiet. When I was alone as a child, I would talk unabashedly to myself, whole long, complex conversations with a cast of characters I had made up. But Salim was silent. He didn't even listen to the radio like Saif did. And, so, Miriam and I would stand there for sometimes two or three minutes or more, our ears pressed on his door. I would become bored and start daydreaming. Miriam would be lost in her own reverie too, I imagine, because we didn't talk to each other or look at each other. More than once the door opened all of a sudden to reveal Salim staring at us. But he would never say, "Get lost!" the way Saif would do when I was bothering him. Nor would he laugh at our shocked faces. He would just walk out to get a Coke or to go to the bathroom, slipping past us as though we didn't exist.

At the dinner table when Miriam told one of her long, animated stories, he appeared to be listening. He smiled—a bit mechanically I thought—when she said something funny. But he didn't contribute anything to the conversation, even as his mother and Miriam peppered him with questions. He would simply shrug or say, "I don't know," even if he must have known the answer to the query being posed, such as who won the hockey game the previous night or if he had any homework left to do that night.

There was, however, at least one occasion during that time when I saw Salim being affectionate with

Miriam and Begum. I had been sitting in the back seat of my family's car in the parking lot of jamat khana after prayers. We were about to go home but my father hadn't started the engine yet for some reason. As I stared out the window, I saw Salim, Miriam, and Begum walking towards Begum's hatchback. Salim said something that made them both laugh. He was walking between them and, after a few moments, he reached out and put his arms around their shoulders, drawing them both closer to him. It was a protective gesture, the type of thing my father might do. I remember thinking I couldn't even imagine Saif doing something like this. My brother and I were equals, jostling for position all the time. Salim seemed beyond Miriam (and me), as though he belonged more in the adult world than in ours. Maybe—I'm wondering this only now—it was because once he became a teenager, he believed he needed to fulfill the role of man of the house, at least of Banting Place. Without a father there, he might have felt more responsibility to be the caretaker. Begum tended to bring this out in her children. As long as I can remember, Miriam had addressed her mother as Begum. Years later, when Miriam was pregnant and we were discussing whether she'd prefer the baby to call her Mummy or Mama, I asked her why she had never called her own mother Mom.

"I don't know," Miriam said, shrugging. "It didn't fit."

Anyways, back then I didn't understand that children might feel forced to take on adult responsibilities, and so I perceived Salim's seriousness as misery. Which is why, one Saturday morning, I asked Miriam why he was so sad all the time.

We had been lying on her bedroom floor under a makeshift tent when I posed this question. One corner of a pale-blue sheet was tied to a bed post and the opposite corner was tied to a chair. We would create this sanctum when we wanted to tell secrets. After I had admitted to stealing a quarter from my mother's nightstand and Miriam looked thoroughly bored, either by the secret I shared (it wasn't the first time I admitted to this transgression) or the manner in which I shared it (it was a rather dull story), we had been silent for a while. Until I brought up Salim.

"He's thirteen," Miriam said. "Teenagers are weird." After a few moments she added, slowly, "Also I think he's upset because of the secret about our dad."

I sat up.

"You cannot tell anyone. This is a super big one."

"I won't," I said, pointing to the sheet above our heads.

Miriam then proceeded to tell me that her father had a secret wife and son in another country. She called it his shadow family. I stared at her. Though Miriam had a tendency to tell dramatic stories, she had never shared anything like this.

"He must be spending his time and money somewhere," she said, by way of explanation.

"But why is it a secret?" A girl in my class had a stepmother who had recently given birth and she never missed an opportunity to talk about her new baby sister.

Miriam shrugged. "Maybe he needs to live a double life for some reason. Maybe in his other life he has a whole different personality and name and job. Like Superman. Except my dad is probably more like two different versions of boring Clark Kent." She was clearly pleased with herself for coming up with this comparison and laughed for quite a long time. But none of it seemed funny to me. I found the idea that a person's father could have an entirely unknown dimension to his life, one involving another family, horrifying.

"Oh, relax," she said, registering the expression I must have had on my face. "There's no shadow family. I'm just pulling your leg."

This was a phrase Miriam had started using lately: "pulling your leg." I thought it was a strange expression and couldn't hear it without picturing a person doing it literally.

"It's just I've been doing a thing lately," she said. "It's called a thought experiment. Do you know what that is?"

I shook my head and Miriam explained that a thought experiment is exactly like it sounds, an experiment you only think; you don't actually test it, usually because you cannot. She was two grades ahead of me and so it didn't occur to me to ask her how she knew about thought experiments. I simply assumed it was something she learned in school.

Oddly, looking back now, I wasn't taught about thought experiments at any point during elementary or secondary school, which makes me wonder if I am conflating older memories with later ones. I don't think so because I can see her, in her bedroom under the blue sheet, saying these words. It might be as simple as Miriam having had an extraordinary grade-school teacher who taught her about thought experiments, or perhaps Salim had told her about them.

She described her thought experiment. "What if we all have another family, a shadow family, that lives in another dimension? This family is identical to ours except for one thing that is different. The different thing for my shadow family is they're white. How would they be living, right now—Begum, Hassan, Salim, and me—as white people?"

"How are they living?" I asked.

"In the other dimension the mom is stylish and beautiful and reads cool books and the dad is an architect and makes his wife giggle because of his bad jokes. They are happily married and live in a very cool house. The son is a football star with loads of girls running around after him," she said. "But he's still weird and doesn't talk much," she added, laughing.

I remember thinking these people sounded a lot like the characters on *The Brady Bunch*, but I didn't say anything because Miriam told me she disliked that show. "The girl, the shadow version of you," I asked, "what's she like?"

"She's brilliant. The teachers love her, and she has skipped so many grades she's in university already."

Then Miriam asked me to do the thought experiment. "What's your white family like?"

I found this thought experiment impossible to do. I couldn't imagine another me that wasn't me. "Does it have to be my family?" I asked. "Can I imagine another four people who are the same ages as my family or something?"

"Obviously, it has to be your family," she said. "Otherwise, you're just making up a story. This is a thought experiment."

My mind couldn't see a version of my life without me in it. Miriam said this was okay; she would keep telling me about her alternate reality where the shadow family had a dog and a big, gorgeous house with two living rooms. I remember that when Miriam was talking about her shadow family, she sounded lighthearted. There had been something hard in the tone of her voice when she spoke of her father earlier in the conversation. It reminded me of the way Saif and I would talk to each other when we were having a terrible fight and I wished he were dead.

Not long after this, I ran into Miriam's father. For about a year Hassan Uncle lived in an apartment building about three kilometres from my family. On this particular occasion I saw him walking on the sidewalk in front of our house. I happened to be outside, though I can't remember precisely what I had been doing. I do recall it was dusk and cold and that I was wearing my brown winter coat and a toque. I was surprised to see him. I had never encountered him like this, without one of my parents or Miriam present. Sometimes he came to our house for dinner, alone, and on those days he would tell me and Saif jokes or he would blow his cigarette smoke into rings and I would reach up and try to catch them. He had never, I am certain, walked to our house. I knew my parents would be delighted to see him and I became excited. I ran towards him, smiling effusively. The smile he returned didn't match mine. Indeed, it was so tepid I felt myself blush. I stopped in front of him and waited for him to walk with me towards our front door. But he remained on the sidewalk.

"Won't you come inside?" I asked.

"Nope. I'm out for an evening stroll."

"But you're here," I said. "You should come in."

"Say hello to your mother and father," he said and turned to walk away. I grabbed his elbow. "Come on!" I said, laughing now. "Come inside."

But he wasn't laughing. Nor was he relenting. He pulled his arm, gently but firmly, out of my hands and kept walking. I couldn't believe he didn't want to come in. I was sure he was playing a game with me. I tugged at his arm again. And again he pulled away. He wasn't angry but he wasn't pleased either. He clearly wasn't playing. But I couldn't stop myself. I threw my arms around him and tried pulling him that way, but he was too strong and broke free. I noticed he did this without much effort, with his hands tucked into his pockets and wearing what I can only describe as a neutral expression on his face. I was nothing more than a mosquito bothering him during, as he put it, his evening stroll. Stunned, I watched him walk away. I went into the house and told my parents what had happened.

My father looked up, but only a for a moment, and resumed staring at the newspaper or whatever it was that he had been reading. "I wonder why he didn't come in?" he added, though his tone didn't convey any genuine curiosity.

My mother looked at me and shrugged.

Neither of them seemed to be surprised by what had happened and so I pushed the incident—and my confusion about it—behind more pressing issues, such as the bubble bath I was planning to have that evening.

A few hours later, my mother came into my bedroom to say goodnight. She lay down next to me in my bed to talk about the day, as she did each night. I told her about my perfect spelling test and how I was afraid I would never learn to skip double dutch. When she was about to get up to leave, I blurted out a question I had not planned to ask her. "Do you think Papa has a shadow family?"

"A shadow family?" she repeated.

"Another family. A second family."

She was quiet for a moment and I watched her face lose some of its colour. "Why would you say such a thing?"

"I don't know. It's a thought experiment." Looking back now, my choice of phrasing that evening was confusing, even to me. It reflected, I realize now, how utterly perplexed I had been by what Miriam had talked about under our makeshift tent.

She furrowed her brow but said nothing. Then she kissed me, stood up, and switched off the light. But she remained in the threshold of my bedroom. "Did Miriam talk to you about this, about," she asked, pausing, "other families?"

My eyes were not yet accustomed to the dark and my mother was nothing more than a shadow. I knew she couldn't see my face, so I lied. "No."

Chapter 3

AS I MENTIONED EARLIER, Begum, Miriam's mother, is a distant relative on my father's side. But unlike Hassan Uncle she never came to our house for dinner. It wasn't explicitly stated that Hassan Uncle was my parents' friend and Begum was not. But when they were talking with her, at a family wedding or such, they seemed to be pretending to be, if not other people, more polished versions of themselves, the way they might behave in a doctor's office or at parent-teacher night at school. When they were with Hassan Uncle, they laughed with their heads thrown back and drank alcohol and ate off one another's plates.

I too had a somewhat distant relationship with Begum. When I was at her house Miriam was always determined to keep us away from her mother. This was easy to do because Begum wasn't interested in me. She didn't notice, for example, that I had grown to be as big as Miriam one year, despite our age difference. Hassan Uncle, on the other hand, commented all the time how tall I was becoming. Which brings up another point. I had addressed Miriam's father as Hassan Uncle for as long as I could recall. Saif and I called all my parents' friends So-and-So Uncle or So-and-So Aunty. Not so in the case of Begum, whom I steadfastly avoided addressing because I knew it was rude for children to address adults by their given names. I once asked my mother why she hadn't taught Saif and me to address Miriam's mother as Begum Aunty, the way she must have done with Hassan Uncle and others.

"Her name isn't Begum," my mother said. "Begum means Lady. It's not a name."

"Why is she called Lady?"

"I heard that when she was in school in Kampala she was in a play and her role was a begum. Her friends must have started calling her Begum back then. And this is how she was introduced to me, as Begum." Then my mother did something funny. She rolled her eyes. "Her name is Roshan," she added. And there the discussion ended, without an answer to my original question. As far as my mother was concerned, it seemed, my relationship with Begum—as well as her own—wasn't terribly important.

And, so, you can imagine how startled I was when I walked into the house after school one day to find

Begum sitting in our living room across from my mother, sipping tea. My mother looked at me and smiled, offering no explanation. I smiled back, said a quick hello to our guest, and went into the kitchen for an after-school snack before retreating to my bedroom. After some time, probably about twenty minutes, I returned to the kitchen for something more to eat. Our house was not large, and I could hear any conversation that was taking place in the living room if I were standing in the kitchen. But Begum and my mother were speaking in low voices, so that if I wanted to listen in on their conversation, I would have had to crawl into the living room and crouch directly beside them. But as I wasn't particularly interested in what they were discussing, I focused on the contents of the refrigerator. I was about to reach for some jam to make a sandwich when I heard a deep-throated, staccato sobbing. For a moment I froze, as though somehow I had been the one responsible for the sound. But it continued. I gently closed the refrigerator door and walked into the living room. Begum was still sitting on the sofa, but her teacup was now on the coffee table in front of her. One of her hands was suspended directly in front of her mouth, the other flat on her chest, and she was crying with abandon, the way a very small child would. My mother had moved to sit beside her and was patting her back, saying, "I know it's hard. I know. I know."

I can't recall how long I was standing there, but at some point Begum, who had not stopped sobbing, looked up and saw me staring at her. But instead of composing herself, which is what I would expect an adult to do, she cried more loudly, without a hint of self-consciousness or embarrassment. My mother made eye contact with me and with a small flick of her head indicated that I should go upstairs, which I was relieved to do.

A half hour or so later, I heard Begum leave. Almost immediately my mother came to my bedroom and told me that Begum "finds her life very difficult" or something to that effect.

"Okay," I said, making myself sound as uninterested as possible. I was feeling acutely embarrassed by what I had witnessed, and I didn't want to talk any more about it.

My mother stood there as though she were considering saying something else. But to my relief she smiled weakly and left. We didn't speak about the incident again.

The next time I saw Miriam, which was about two weeks later, I told her that her mother had been crying very loudly in my living room the other day. She turned to look at me, surprised, the colour draining from her face. Then she looked down again. We had been setting up a checkerboard on my dining room table. "Oh, Begum," she said, shaking her head. "She thinks her life is a movie."

The dissonance between Miriam's nonchalant words and the sudden blanching of her skin confused me. I noticed too that though she was moving pieces on the checkerboard she was doing so with no purpose. She was just sliding one piece against another, making a *tick tick tick* sound. I don't know why I told Miriam about her mother; maybe I wanted to show that I knew something she didn't, which happened so rarely then. But now I felt terrible for having brought it up. "You know," I said. "Maybe it wasn't that bad. I think she was crying only a little bit. Like my mom does sometimes."

Miriam looked at me as though she wanted nothing more in her life than to believe me. She forced a smile and held it until the colour returned to her face. Then she placed the pieces properly on the checkerboard. In a few minutes she was herself again, back to telling me what to do and how to do it. I was grateful. We didn't discuss Begum's crying jag again.

Another curious incident involving Begum occurred at Banting Place, when I was there for a sleepover. This must have happened—in fact I'm sure it did—before the crying episode, but I am reminded of it now because I had cause to mention Begum not noticing how much I had grown.

Whenever I would ask my mother if I could sleep over at a school friend's house she would say a variation of the following: "What if something happens to you? It's not safe. Something could happen." None of this made any sense to me. What could happen? And why would it happen only when I was sleeping over at some-one's house? She would not entertain my questions, nor would she budge. And, so, though Miriam slept over at our house multiple times, I didn't ask if I could sleep over at hers. Then one Saturday morning my mother stunned me by announcing that I would be going to Miriam's house that afternoon to spend the night.

"Why?" I asked.

"Because you have been invited. Don't you want to go?"

"Yes! I want to go!" I said quickly. "But you said no—"

"Miriam is family," she said, interrupting me. "It's different."

It was different. In my childhood thereafter, just as before, I would never be allowed to sleep over at any school friend's houses. Only family. Only—because I was not friends with any of my cousins—Miriam's house.

After lunch my father dropped me off at Banting Place. I stood at the front door, wearing blue jeans, a matching jean jacket over a T-shirt, and stained white sneakers. I remember the outfit because, never having been to a sleepover, I had taken a great deal of care selecting my clothes. The jeans were my very own, not a hand-me-down pair from Saif. And the T-shirt, white with red piping and three small flowers embroidered onto the front, had been part of a ninth-birthday gift from my parents. I would have liked new shoes but of course this was impossible. Mine still fit. In my right hand I was carrying the same little grey vinyl suitcase

(Saif had an identical one) I had brought on my flight to Canada two years earlier. Inside the suitcase was a neatly folded pair of pyjamas and my toothbrush. Miriam grabbed my suitcase and we raced up the stairs to her bedroom. She set my suitcase on the floor beside her bed, where a comforter and pillow were laid out for me already, as she described everything that she had planned for the next twenty-four hours, including making pancakes for breakfast and sneaking into Salim's room. Miriam explained to me that she was convinced her brother, who was acting strange lately, even for a teenager, was "on drugs." I didn't know what "on drugs" meant except that it was something horrible. Rather than ruining the moment by asking too many questions I nodded enthusiastically. But we needed to wait until he was out of the house. First, she said, we were going to walk to the convenience store nearby to stock up on candy. "I have a whole dollar," she added.

Only two minutes into our walk, it started to rain. We sprinted, hoping to reach the store before we were too wet. But it was a good kilometre and a half away and the rain was coming down in sheets. We were drenched. Miriam pointed in the direction of Banting Place and we turned and ran home.

I WAS STANDING in the shower, warm water cascading over me, imagining it was a waterfall when I remembered I was at Miriam's house and she was waiting to use the bathtub. I quickly rinsed the remainder of the shampoo out of my hair, turned off the tap, pulled open the shower curtain, and stepped out. The mat was soaking wet. It had become very steamy in the bathroom but I couldn't imagine that I had created enough steam to soak the mat like this. I looked around and saw that the entire bathroom floor was covered with water. I tried mopping it up with my towel but there was too much. I put on a bathrobe that had been hanging on a hook, opened the door and called for Miriam. As I did so, I noticed that the water was seeping into the carpet in the hallway.

Miriam quickly ascertained that while showering I had left the shower curtain on the outside of the bathtub. At my house we had shower doors, not a curtain, and her explanation confused me. She stepped closer to the tub to show me how the water coming from the shower would have run along the curtain and onto the floor. "You need to make sure the curtain is on the inside of the tub when you shower. If you're having a bath, you leave it on the outside so it's not in the bath with you."

She was extraordinarily patient as she explained this to me, considering I had created a substantial puddle in her bathroom.

This reminds me how years later, when we were in university, Miriam explained what an event horizon is by comparing a black hole to an infinite bathtub with a drain in the middle.

"The closer you get to the drain, the faster the water moves," she said. "At some point the water is moving so fast, nothing can resist being pulled down the drain. That point is called the event horizon."

"What happens after that?" I asked.

"Eventually the current is so fast that not even light speed is fast enough to swim against it. When light passes across the current it gets swept downstream a little, off course basically. The current makes light change course the way a lens makes light change course. So, when you look at the stars beyond a black hole, it looks like there's an invisible lens in the way. Sometimes there are rings of light."

I thought a black hole sounded horrifying. Miriam had a different take.

"I sometimes imagine going into one," she had said that day. "As I approach the event horizon, I'm surrounded by a stream of blinding light. And then darkness washes over me as I approach singularity. After that, who knows. But until then? Wow."

But this was much later, after Miriam had begun to study physics. That day at Banting Place, Miriam and I were—more or less silently—doing our best to clean up the mess I had made. Begum arrived as I was standing in the middle of the bathroom, mopping, and Miriam was on her knees in the hallway soaking up water with a towel. After Miriam described what had happened, I added a heartfelt "I'm sorry."

Begum was surveying the room and ignored me.

"Oh, don't worry," Miriam replied, though she must have known I was speaking to her mother because I used a high-pitched tone, the one that seemed to come out of my mouth when speaking to adults. "This happens all the time."

"No, it doesn't," said Begum, sounding genuinely confused. "It has never happened." Miriam had been dabbing a towel on the drenched hallway carpet quickly, as though she wanted to erase my mistake as fast as possible. But when her mother spoke, she stopped and became completely still. In a moment Begum shook her head and walked out, and Miriam resumed her dabbing.

By the next day, the rain had stopped and Miriam and I set out to the convenience store again. For some reason that I couldn't fathom, Miriam decided to ride her bicycle alongside me as I walked. When she took it out of the garage, I noticed it was missing its right pedal and asked her how she could possibly ride it like that.

"Oh, it's totally fine. Watch." She proceeded to ride around the driveway in a large oblong. On the non-pedal side, she was able to push her right foot down on the metal crank arm but had to wait for that side to come up again, so that she looked awkward and unstable. She reminded me of a circus bear I'd seen on television. Despite my protests she was deter-mined to ride and off we went. Because our speeds were mismatched, she was forced to ride her bicycle around me in circles. And because she wanted to carry on a conversation, she had to keep her circles relatively small. She was teetering the whole time. On the way home, her balancing act became even more precarious because she was holding a Tootsie Roll in her right hand, periodically taking bites. When we reached the Banting Place complex, Miriam suddenly veered to avoid a pothole, causing her to lose control and head straight towards me. I shifted to my right, but she moved to the same side. I shifted to my left, and she mirrored me again. This was not deliberate on either of our parts. We were making split-second decisions to avoid a collision, though in my memory it happened in slow motion. I watched Miriam coming towards me, clearly out of control and trying desperately to avoid me. Though I knew she didn't want to hurt me (indeed, she was trying very much to avoid hurting me), I felt an uncomfortable sensation, as though I were being betrayed. As though I were watching the act of betrayal play out but was powerless to stop it. When she crashed into me, she knocked me to the ground and landed, along with her bicycle, on top of me. She apologized repeatedly as she helped me up.

For a few moments I felt very sorry for myself. My clothes were soaked and I had a deep gash on the top of my wrist. But I didn't cry or shout at Miriam as I would have done if Saif had knocked me over. Instead I muttered an insincere "It's okay" and even managed a smile when I noticed Miriam was still holding her Tootsie Roll. She giggled and offered me a bite, which

I declined, and promised with great flourish to put her bicycle in the dumpster tomorrow, which of course she would not do, and which I would not want her to do.

I washed my wrist in the bathroom sink and then placed the two Band-Aids Miriam had given me on it. In hindsight we should have visited the emergency room. The gash left a small oval-shaped scar. But looking at it now I'm grateful I didn't receive any stitches. Without this mark on my flesh I would have no proof that those days had ever happened.

A few minutes later Miriam was rifling through her drawers to find something for me to wear when Begum walked into her bedroom.

"How can she wear your clothes?" Begum asked after Miriam explained what she was doing. "They will be too big."

"Look at her," Miriam said, laughing. "And then look at me."

We stood by side and Begum did as her daughter asked, her eyes resting first on me, then Miriam. "She is younger than you," she said, with a hint of irritation in her voice, as though this fact overrode the reality that we were precisely the same height and build.

When I emerged downstairs a little while later wearing Miriam's brown corduroy pants and yellow pullover sweater, all of which fit perfectly, Begum glanced at me so briefly I'm not sure she saw me. Anyways, she said nothing.

Chapter 4

UNLIKE BEGUM, Hassan Uncle's new girlfriend noticed changes in me, like how tall I was getting or that I had my hair trimmed. The first time she remarked on my appearance, or I suppose the first time I took notice of her doing so, was at our house. Leigh Ann had come over with Hassan Uncle and Miriam and Salim for dinner. She had been to our house before; by that point I think I had met her three or maybe four times. On this particular occasion, as soon as she saw me enter the living room—she had been in a conversation with my father at the time, I believe—she turned and exclaimed, "Oh I love how you parted your hair today." I was ten and beginning to make an effort with my appearance, a minor and inconsistent effort, mind you. I would still regularly go to school with greasy hair or mismatched socks. But once in a while, say if we were going out to a nice restaurant or to jamat khana for a special holiday, I would put on a pair of small hoop earrings and tie my hair in a high ponytail. The day Leigh Ann commented on my hair I had left it down. But it was washed and brushed and I had decided to part it on the side instead of the middle as I usually did. No one in my family remarked on it, not even my mother. Although, that's not entirely true. My mother did say it looked nice, but only after she heard Leigh Ann say what she did.

After that, whenever I saw Leigh Ann, at our house usually but sometimes at Waterloo Park or Laurel Creek for a barbecue, I would run up and say hello. She would always look pleased to see me, as though she'd been waiting for me to show up. When she asked me questions, I didn't have the sense that she was doing so to be polite. She seemed genuinely interested in what I had to say.

It occurs to me that over the years I have thought of Leigh Ann a great deal, more often, certainly, than any other person who briefly wandered into my childhood. As I think about it now, I'm not sure there was anything all that special about her. I suspect the more likely reason she left such a deep impression on me is because of what happened later. The fact is, I had no more than ten conversations with Leigh Ann before she was gone from our lives.

We talked most often about Judy Blume books.

"Of course, she likes children's books," my mother said when I told her about our shared interest at dinner one night. "She's a child."

"She's twenty-one," my father said. "You were married and had a baby by that age."

"She's half his age."

"He's happy. Let's be happy for him." I detected some impatience in the tone of my father's voice when he said this. His words seemed to be a command rather than something we might all consider doing. He was looking down, focused on eating, appearing to enjoy his meal. My mother's eyes were on her plate too, but she was angry. I could see her blinking quickly and her jaw was set. I knew she didn't like Leigh Ann. My mother's body became visibly stiff every time she was nearby. Whenever she addressed Leigh Ann directly, her words sounded hollow, as though she were an actress who didn't believe the lines she was delivering. My father, on the other hand, clearly enjoyed Leigh Ann's company, laughing at her jokes and listening intently when she was speaking. He would also use her name frequently. I think he found it easy to pronounce and so he enjoyed saying it. "Leigh Ann, let me tell you ..." or "Leigh Ann, you must know this ..." It's entirely possible my mother was jealous of the attention he was giving her. Miriam didn't like Leigh Ann either. I knew for certain she was jealous of the attention Hassan Uncle was giving his girlfriend.

"My dad never wants to go out with us, his own kids," Miriam said once, out of the blue. "But he is so excited to go out with her."

"He goes out with you," I said. Miriam had plenty of time with her father, I was sure of it. Dinners, weekends, and holidays together. She had far more alone time with her father than I had with mine.

"But he doesn't want to. He has to because it's his scheduled time with us."

I thought Miriam was being ridiculous, so I decided it was best to say nothing further. As far as I can recall the subject was dropped that day.

The thing is, Hassan Uncle had girlfriends over the years and Miriam had never reacted like this. To be fair, none of his previous relationships had become this serious. Leigh Ann had been on holiday (to Kenya) with Hassan Uncle, and she regularly came to our house. She had developed an easy familiarity with all of us, as though she were a family member, a cousin or something. Her long, straight black hair helped her blend in.

"She dyes her hair that shoe polish colour," Miriam told me once, "in the bathroom sink."

At the time I didn't believe her. I knew Miriam disliked Leigh Ann, so I assumed she was looking for ways to diminish her. But looking back on it when I was older and had a better understanding of colouring and that type of thing—Leigh Ann had porcelain-white skin and light blue eyes, framed by fair eyebrows—it was pretty obvious she used to dye her hair.

As I was saying, Leigh Ann was comfortable in our house. She would help my mother set the table and she always took the lead in clearing up afterwards. She was at ease with my father too. She would do things like gently touch his back when she was talking or place her hand on his forearm to get his attention.

Salim liked her as well, I know, because he smiled when she was around, which is something he rarely did. Once I saw them talking in our backyard. It must have been summer because they were standing by the raspberry bush and I remember thinking I should tell them to move away because there are always bees hovering around that bush. But something stopped me. Maybe it was the way they were standing, with their backs to everyone else. Or it might have been the way their heads were leaning into each other, creating a sort of closed-off space. I could have been mistaken; they might have welcomed an interruption. Of course, I'll never know. At the time, seeing them like this reminded me how easy Leigh Ann was to talk to, even for someone like Salim.

She was sweet with Miriam too. But Miriam wouldn't try at all. She would answer her questions with a word or maybe two and wander away. I don't know what it was like when they were alone, without my family around. It must have been uncomfortable for everyone. But I never saw Leigh Ann look annoyed with Miriam.

One time, about a year after Hassan Uncle had first

introduced us to Leigh Ann, our two families went to a restaurant for his birthday. After he blew out his candles, Leigh Ann placed her palms on either side of his face and turned his head towards her. In front of everyone, they kissed on the mouth. This was not something my parents or anyone's parents that I knew ever did, but it wasn't that big a deal. It was only a peck. My mother was, as you can imagine, horrified. She talked about it in the car the whole way home.

At bedtime when she was lying with me, she was still talking about it. "She is so forward. This girl is a trickster," she said. She was speaking a mixture of Punjabi and English and used a Punjabi idiom that doesn't translate too well. Literally it is this: "That woman is going to eat him up." I think a better way to convey it in English is to say: "That woman will have him for breakfast." I think you get the point. My mother ended her tirade, finally, by announcing that she was going to tell Hassan Uncle this the next time she saw him. "I will," she insisted, though I had said nothing. "I'm going to tell him she will make a fool of him."

It was an empty threat. My mother would never say anything negative about Leigh Ann to Hassan Uncle. She didn't talk to men in that way. She answered their questions or politely asked after their wives or children, but nothing beyond pleasantries. I had never seen her say anything that might make a man upset or unhappy. This included my father. For example, my father used to blow his nose and leave the dirty Kleenexes lying around the house, on the sofa, on the coffee table. Instead of asking him to pick them up she would wait until he was out of the room and mutter, "I wish people in this house would pick up their own messes," as she picked up his.

Come to think of it, being agreeable, in particular being agreeable with men, was a matter of pride with my mother. She told me, more than once, that women should lower their eyes in the presence of men. "It's attractive," she said. I agreed with her then, about a lot of things to do with women and how they should behave, but especially about that. For many years I believed submission was a desirable trait in a woman. Miriam thought this was ridiculous, and I suppose this explains a lot about our respective relationships when we were older. But I'll come to all that later. First I need to get to the reason why I am telling you about Leigh Ann, a woman who did not, as it happens, lower her eyes in the presence of men.

What happened is Leigh Ann became pregnant. Miriam found out about it because she was snooping in her purse and saw a pregnancy test kit. I remember the day she told me about it. I was excited because a baby would mean Leigh Ann would marry Hassan Uncle and stay in our lives. I was so happy I didn't pick up at all how upset Miriam was. Thinking about it now, I don't think Miriam wanted to tell me about the pregnancy test at all. She had been quiet the whole afternoon until I asked her if she was feeling sick or something. Immediately after she told me what she had discovered, she sat on the floor of my bedroom slumped over, as though some force were pushing her downwards, and fiddled with some loose threads in my carpet. She looked up at me at one point and said she would confront her father right away, tomorrow in fact, when he was supposed to pick her up from her school.

She reported details of the conversation to me the following Friday at jamat khana.

She had asked her father outright if he was having a baby with Leigh Ann. At first, he didn't say he was or wasn't. Instead, he asked Miriam how she'd feel about a little brother or sister. Miriam started to cry and said it was a horrible idea. He didn't care about his kids who were already born and living; why would he want another one? He told Miriam that of course he cared and seemed genuinely upset that she didn't know this. This softened Miriam quite a bit, she told me. Then they talked about other things for a while, like what teachers Miriam liked best and where they should go on holiday next summer. By the end, she told me, her dad said he was going to break up with Leigh Ann because he was over her. I asked her what she meant by that.

"He said stuff like they are different people and she'll find a guy her age and this was only a fun relationship."

"What about the baby?" I asked.

"There's no baby," Miriam said. When he was about to leave, he said: *You saw a test, Miriam. That's all.* "Anyways," Miriam added, and I remember this more clearly than any other part of the conversation because of her expression. It was a look of self-satisfaction, or maybe of conquest, the expression that would settle on her face when she won an argument against me or was in some other way proven right. "He said I was more important than anyone. He said his focus needed to be only on me right now."

I thought Miriam was being kind of a spoiled brat but of course I couldn't say this, so instead I said, "Salim will be disappointed. He seemed to really like Leigh Ann."

For years I have regretted these words. If I hadn't said them maybe Miriam wouldn't have told Salim. But, of course, this makes no sense. Her telling Salim was a completely natural thing to do. She would have told him, if not that day, a few days later. But she didn't tell him later. She told him right away, that night.

Salim wanted to know how she found out their father was going to break up with Leigh Ann. So she told him about everything, the pregnancy test and the conversation. Miriam told me Salim became really upset. He was breathing heavily, pacing back and forth in the living room and scratching his head with both hands compulsively as though he had lice or fleas. Miriam felt badly and explained to Salim that their father wanted to focus on her *and* him, that she only forgot to mention his name earlier. This was a lie, but she was panicked. Miriam said she'd never seen him like that. He left the house for about a half hour and came back home and went straight into his bedroom. He didn't come out when Miriam knocked on his door. He just asked her, politely she said, to leave him alone for a while. Later that same night, after Miriam and Begum were asleep, Salim took his mother's car and drove off. He was only fifteen and didn't have a driver's licence, but Hassan Uncle had taught him how to drive on their weekends together, so sometimes he would take the car to the nearby convenience store. But this time he was going farther (though no one knows where) because he took the expressway. Unfortunately, it was snowing heavily and Salim lost control of the car and hit a truck that had broken down on the side of the road. He didn't die right away. He died the next day at the hospital, with his parents and Miriam in the room with him.

Chapter 5

M

Y PARENTS HAD an argument the day after Salim's funeral. This wasn't terribly unusual. Throughout my childhood they would argue once in a while, usually in their bedroom after they thought Saif and I were asleep. They didn't shout so much as volley words back and forth at a quick pace. I could never make out what they were saying and, for the most part, I wasn't very interested. But these closed-door arguments were the exception. More typically when they had disagreements they didn't discuss them as much as act on them. This was because of my mother's reluctance, as I explained earlier, to be confrontational with men. If she was upset with my father and couldn't fix the situation (say, by picking up those dirty Kleenexes) she would be cold with him (curt answers, no eye contact) but overly sweet with Saif and me (attentive, even doting), to clarify—in case it wasn't obvious—that it was my father only with whom she was upset. My father would respond by becoming irritable and impatient, finding fault with seemingly everything (my mother's cooking, school bags in the front hallway, the sound of our laughter).

The argument after the funeral was different. For one thing I had a front row seat to watch it. The second thing is my mother was acting strangely. She was forthright with my father, demanding even. I suppose her behaviour could be attributed to the timing; everyone's emotions were heightened for obvious reasons. But, still, it surprised me.

That morning my mother had awoken with a headache and asked me to iron a sari. (We would be attending jamat khana that evening.) I don't know if you have ever ironed a sari, but it isn't an easy thing to do. Saris are six yards long and usually made of a slippery fabric that obviously cannot all fit on an ironing table. As I would iron one portion, the rest—pulled down by the force of gravity—would gather in a clump on the floor so that no matter how much I kept at it, I couldn't seem to get the whole thing pressed. At the best of times, I loathed this particular job. On this day I was feeling even more put out because I could hear Saif in the other room watching television and chomping on some snack or another. After only a few minutes of effort I gave up. I folded the still wrinkled sari, hanging it on my forearm as my mother had taught me to do, and headed up the stairs.

Before I continue, I should explain a bit about the layout of our house. The ironing board was kept in the laundry room, which was in the unfinished part of our basement. To reach the stairs you needed to walk through the finished part, where we kept the television, a sofa, and an armchair. Those stairs led up to the kitchen; but before you entered the kitchen, there was a landing. To the right of the landing was the door to the garage and to the left, the door to the kitchen. Because Saif had the television on that morning, I didn't hear my parents until I was almost at the top of the stairs. By the time I reached the landing, I had detected—by how low and clipped their voices were—that my mother and father were having an argument. The door into the kitchen was slightly ajar, so that I could see my parents each in profile. If either of them turned towards the door, they would have seen me easily. But they never did. It was apparent from their body language—my mother's back was straight and her arms were folded against her chest while my father looked more relaxed, with one hand resting on the back of a chair—that my mother was angry but my father was less so.

"But why you?" my mother asked. I was shocked by her tone because it was, as I say, unusually forthright.

My father didn't reply. He was shaking his head and laughing dismissively, the way you might do with a small child who was being silly.

"Why?" she said again and then again. "Why?"

My father, to my surprise, didn't show any signs of being irritated at all while she pressed him. Finally, he said, "Ishrat, you are making too much of nothing. She was in trouble. She knows no one here—"

"She could have called me. Doesn't a woman ask another woman for this type of help?"

"She should have asked you for help?" Now my father laughed openly.

My mother's face became contorted. She looked physically sick with rage. Almost immediately he stopped laughing. They had been conversing up to now, as they usually did, in Gujarati. My father's family was Gujarati and though my mother's was Punjabi she was fluent in Gujarati, having learned it in school and in jamat khana. My father, on the other hand, did not speak Punjabi. I'm explaining this to you now because at this point, my mother did something odd. She spoke in English. "What kind of a woman asks a man to help her get an abortion?" Because she asked this question in a language that didn't come as easily to her as Gujarati or Punjabi, it sounded stilted, performed even. For a second I was confused. I thought she was talking about a television show. Once, a few months or maybe even a year earlier, my mother and I were watching TV in the afternoon. The main character, who was old with greying hair and grown children, had become pregnant. The whole episode was about whether or not she should get an abortion, which, it quickly became obvious to me, meant to end the pregnancy before the baby had really formed.

As I watched my parents now, it was quiet, with the exception of my mother's heavy breathing. "Tell me," she said and then switched to Gujarati again. "Make me understand." Her words came from deep in her throat, as though she were going hoarse. It was clear my mother wasn't talking about a television show.

But my father said nothing. I don't remember exactly how he left the kitchen, whether he waved his hand like it didn't matter or he just walked out, but in a moment he was gone.

Looking back, I should have realized they were discussing Leigh Ann. When Miriam told me that Leigh Ann wasn't pregnant, I didn't believe it, or at the very least I doubted it was true. Miriam was extremely upset when she confronted her father—she'd never admitted crying to him about anything before—so I could imagine Hassan Uncle saying whatever it took to calm her down. And, so, knowing how much my mother disapproved of Leigh Ann, I couldn't blame her for being upset that Leigh Ann felt comfortable asking my father to take her to get an abortion when she, his own wife, couldn't ask him to pick up after himself. None of this matters. I was oblivious that my parents were arguing about Leigh Ann until a few weeks later, when I pieced it together during a conversation with Miriam.

Back on the landing I closed my eyes and counted to twenty in my head before walking into the kitchen so that my mother would not suspect I had heard any of their argument. When I entered, she was sitting at the kitchen table, rubbing her temples with the thumb and index finger of one hand. She turned to me and stared, as though I were an alien or a ghost who had suddenly materialized. Her face looked altered. The angry woman demanding answers from my father moments ago was gone. In her place was my mother, looking exhausted and defeated. You know when a basketball player on television is cocky and acting like he's the greatest player ever because every shot he takes goes in? But then in the last few minutes of the game he fails to make some really easy baskets and his team ends up losing and he looks small, like he's been cut down to size in front of everyone? And even though he's cocky, you can't help but feel sorry for him? That's how I felt looking at my mother.

"I didn't do a very good job," I said, handing her the sari.

She smiled, took the sari, and briefly took my hand in hers. Then she stood up and went downstairs.

I'm reminded of something about my mother just now. I was sitting next to her at Salim's funeral. But I was staring at Miriam. She had her arm around her mother's shoulders—which seemed to have shrunk in the hours since Salim died—holding her firmly. Begum was slumped over and crying into her hands, and Miriam was stoic and sitting tall so that she looked like the parent and Begum the child. Salim was lying in a casket only a few feet away, its lid propped open. Hassan Uncle was directly in front of the casket, facing it, and behind him sat my father and Saif. The seven of us, eight if you count Salim (and why shouldn't we count Salim?), were like pieces of driftwood on a sea of people. The entire Kitchener jamat was there. Everyone was packed, shoulder to shoulder, into that funeral home on King Street. The people who worked there must have laid carpets down so we could sit on the floor, as we did in jamat khana. Incense was burning and I was stifled by its smell, by the heat of all the bodies around me, by the overwhelming and relentless sadness.

"Can I go outside?" I shouldn't have asked. Miriam had no choice but to endure all this. Poor Salim had died. I waited for my mother to mutter something in Punjabi, to tell me off for being so childish. But she didn't look annoyed at all. Instead, she gently nudged me with her elbow towards the door as though it had been her idea. "Go. Wait in the hall," she whispered. "It's okay."

IN THE WEEKS after Salim died, I wasn't able to spend any meaningful time with Miriam. I would see her at jamat khana—my family went every evening for the full forty-day mourning period—but she was busy looking after Begum for the most part. At Banting Place she was surrounded by aunts and uncles and cousins and a stream of visitors. After we had stopped by two or three times, my mother thought it best for us to stay away.

After the mourning period, Hassan Uncle left for an extended business trip. ("He has run off," my mother said, adding, "poor man.") Begum's sister was staying at Banting Place for a few more weeks and so Miriam started coming to our house on the occasional weekend to sleep over. When she was with us, you could not have guessed that she had buried her brother only weeks ago. We would watch television and eat Kentucky Fried Chicken and laugh about things as though nothing had changed.

She directly addressed Salim's death only once. We were sitting at the top of a hill near my house. It was an unseasonably warm day in March. I remember that I had unzipped my coat. I think we must have been tobogganing earlier because that's the only time we went to that particular hill, though I don't remember the tobogganing part at all. I do recall that at one point we both lay on our backs and stared at the sky. It was overcast, the clouds varying shades of grey.

"Where is he?" she asked. We had been quiet for a while before she had spoken. The way she said it, or maybe because she couldn't have meant anyone else in that moment, I knew she was talking about Salim.

I didn't know how to answer because I didn't know. I turned to look at her.

"Where did he go?" She sat up and looked at me. For a second I thought she really believed I knew, that maybe she thought I was hiding him or something.

I sat up as well. "Isn't he in heaven?" I asked.

She was staring at me but her mind seemed to have gone somewhere else. "Do you know that thing when you learn a word and then you hear that word all the time for the next few days?"

"I think so," I replied. "Yes."

"Maybe we make our own reality. Maybe if I accept he's dead, he'll stay dead. But if I let myself believe he's not, I'll see him."

Can she really have said *we make our own reality*? I can't believe she said that when she was twelve. This is the type of thing Miriam talked about later, a great deal, when she was an adult. I fear I'm informing my earlier memories with later ones. But it doesn't matter, because the gist of this memory is accurate. She did suggest she could believe Salim into existence. She was convincing. I actually thought she could do it and found myself nodding enthusiastically. Then my mind tripped on some logic.

"How?" I asked. I knew she had been with him when he died. She saw him die. My mother told me this. And at the funeral we all saw him in his casket. His face was perfect, his cheeks flushed and his lips a soft pink, but that face looked more like a mask than the boy I had known for as long as I could remember. "How can you make yourself believe he's alive?"

She was shaking her head. "Simple. I won't believe my eyes. Our eyes can trick us. Look at magicians. They

66

do it all the time. Anyways, my mind doesn't believe he's gone forever from everywhere. It doesn't. I try to believe it and my mind says no. *No way.* When my mom makes me go to his grave, I won't look at it. I'll look up at the sky or something."

We didn't talk about this plan anymore that day. It didn't work, of course. She accepted his death eventually. But I suppose this way of thinking is what got her through the worst of her grief.

As I was saying, it was during a conversation with Miriam that I figured out it had been Leigh Ann my parents were arguing about. It wasn't during this conversation on the hill, but it was on that same weekend, either that night or the next. It was late and we were in my basement watching television. I can't recall where my parents and Saif were. We had been watching a show—I can no longer remember which one—but a young woman came onscreen. She had long, straight black hair and blue eyes and we must have both thought the same thing, that she looked like Leigh Ann, because Miriam suddenly said that she had been surprised Leigh Ann hadn't been at the funeral.

"But then my dad told me she was sick," Miriam said. "She had to go to the hospital. She's okay, but that's why she couldn't come. Still," she went on, "you'd think she'd have come around to see us after."

This is the moment when I put it together. And I said this: "She had an abortion. Is that what you mean by her being sick?" I don't know why I said it like that.

Of course, this isn't what Miriam meant. If she had meant abortion, she would have said abortion.

She stared at me. "What are you talking about? She wasn't pregnant."

"She was. I overheard my parents talking about it after the funeral."

In her silence, Miriam didn't look angry. She looked as though she were trying to sort out a puzzle or a mystery. "He said she had a procedure," she said after a few moments. "That's what my dad said. He didn't say hospital at all. He said she had to go for a procedure and she was resting." She stared at me for a while, saying nothing. It felt like that look lasted a whole minute, though it can't have been that long. She continued. "But on the day of Salim's funeral? Did she have to do it on that very day?"

"It wasn't on that day," I said. "It was before. I'm sure of it. My dad took her. And he was with us the whole day of the funeral. It had to be before."

We didn't discuss it any further, not until Miriam brought it up a decade later.

It was about a year before Miriam moved to Toronto for grad school. I was already living there, doing my undergraduate degree at the University of Toronto. Begum was living in Don Mills at that point, and Miriam was visiting her mother in the middle of term because she was having minor surgery for something I can't recall. Miriam and I were in the kitchen of a rambling, rundown century home in the Annex, attending a party. It was one of those university house parties where there are about fifteen or twenty people spread out in various rooms, drinking and talking in small groups, so that it's not a party in the true sense of the word. Sometimes one or two people wandered into the kitchen to get something from the fridge, but mostly Miriam and I were alone. We had brought some beer and she had finished a can and had opened a second by then. I hadn't even finished one because beer tends to upset my stomach.

For the past week, Miriam had been convinced she was pregnant. She would phone me and moan about how she had been planning to break up with her boyfriend and what would she do now? Would it be fair to get an abortion without telling him? What would happen? I told her more than once to do a pregnancy test to find out if it were even true instead of carrying on like this. It's all she talked about and it was getting pretty annoying. Finally, she agreed. But before she bought the test, she started her period. She was so relieved she wanted to go out and have some fun, so we decided to come here. I don't know if it was the beer or the dull party but she was unusually quiet the whole evening. I was about to say I wanted to head home when she brought it up. "Do you think Leigh Ann aborted the baby because of me? Because I threw a tantrum?"

It had been so long since I heard that name that I was a bit taken aback. I even took a large sip of beer to avoid responding, which made me feel slightly sick. "They split up," I said, finally. "She was really young and didn't want a baby then. It wasn't because of you."

She was nodding and kept nodding. The gesture wasn't indicating she agreed with me. It was more akin to the way you might shake your leg when you're nervous. "Everything changed because I found that pregnancy test and flipped out on my dad. Salim. My dad getting messed up. Us moving to Burnaby. My mom marrying that asshole. Everything."

How do you know everything changed? How do you know everything didn't play out exactly as it would have if you hadn't snooped? We aren't children anymore. You aren't the centre of the universe. This is what I wanted to say. But I wasn't sure she was wrong. So, I said nothing.

Chapter 6

SEVEN MONTHS AFTER Salim died, Begum and Miriam were living in Burnaby. "Begum wants a fresh start," Miriam had told me when she announced the move a few weeks before they left. She was understandably upset about her mother's decision but refused to discuss it with me.

Whenever I asked anything related to the move— "Have you packed? Are you taking your bike? Are you sad about leaving?"—she shrugged. And she had a real pout on her face when she did. She had a pout on her face most of the time those days. I have to admit she had become really unpleasant. For example, let's say we were watching television and I made an observation I thought was clever. She would turn to me and make a face like it was the dumbest thing anyone had

71

ever said. And in case I didn't fully grasp her disgust, she would roll her eyes. At the playground she would suddenly become quiet and say absolutely nothing— even if I asked a direct question—for the longest time. It got to the point that I didn't want to be around her.

My mother more or less forced me to spend time with her then. "She has lost so much," she told me. "Be patient with her."

This behaviour of Miriam's went on until they moved.

The strange thing is, years later at Begum's funeral when Miriam and I talked about how suddenly they moved to Burnaby after Salim's death, she insisted she had been completely unbothered by the move. In fact, she said she had been glad they were moving because it was good for Begum to live near her sister; this took pressure off Miriam. But I don't remember it that way at all. I think Miriam blocked it out of her mind, the way she had acted back then. It was a painful period of transition for her and I'm not surprised she didn't want to face it. She did allude to the pain of that move once, though, now that I think of it. When she was pregnant with Zara, she had Salim's telescope repaired. It was the only thing of his she had kept and she wanted to give it to her child. What I'm recalling about this incident is how dejected she looked as she held the telescope in her hands.

"I had to pick something from his room to keep," she said. "One big thing or a bunch of small things. And everything else would be thrown out or given away like his existence was nothing. I stood in there for the longest time. It was like someone asked me to grab hold of the essence of him and walk away with it, like that could ever be done. I was about to walk out with nothing and then I saw his telescope near the window. So, I took it." She moved it around in her hands a bit, almost as though she were nervous about what she was going to say. "But I'm glad I did, because when I look through it—I mean it's such a silly little toy and I've seen through some of the most powerful telescopes on the planet—it's like I'm seeing what he saw. I'm seeing his perspective, looking out the window from that room of his at Banting Place, you know, overlooking the parking lot. And when I do, he's here." She held her hand flat against her chest.

It occurs to me I have no idea where that telescope, or indeed anything of Miriam's, is. It's as though all traces of her and her family have been erased from the earth.

Shortly before she moved to Burnaby, Miriam told me that she would thereafter travel to Kitchener each summer to spend her vacations with her father. I expected, therefore, that our friendship would remain largely unchanged. With the exception of the period after Salim's death, Miriam and I rarely saw each other during the winter months, when we were both busy with school and sports teams and such. So when she didn't telephone me from Burnaby that first winter or respond to the letter I sent her, I didn't give it a thought. Okay, that's not completely true. I was a little surprised I didn't hear from her after I'd written a whole letter. But I was old enough to understand—and my mother reminded me often—that Miriam had been through a lot of disruption. She was very busy settling into a new house and a new school; her silence was to be expected. I told myself that as soon as the school year ended everything would go back to normal.

When Miriam did return to Kitchener for the summer, however, it was clear something had changed. The first time I saw her, in the parking lot at jamat khana, I ran towards her with a broad smile on my face. "Hi!" I said.

Though she was standing alone and had no reason to be distracted, she acted as though she hadn't heard me, her eyes unfocused and staring off to the side. I shifted my body slightly to where I thought she was looking and for a second, less than a second really, our eyes met. Just as quickly she turned and walked away. In my confusion I called out her name, but she didn't stop.

This happened a few more times over that summer. I didn't run up to her ever again, certainly. But sometimes after Friday prayers, I would stand and wait for her to notice me, pull me into a conversation or a game—as she used to do. Instead, she continued to behave as though I were invisible. In hindsight and in the context of all the decades of our friendship, this strange behaviour didn't last long; it only went on for that one summer, mere weeks. But I felt so thoroughly eradicated that it seemed—during my childhood and for many years beyond—as though that year were an epoch. A sad and heavy epoch.

Miriam had a different recollection. About a decade later, when she was living in Vancouver and I was in Toronto, I asked her about the year she had ignored me. At the time, she was accusing me of not replying to a letter quickly enough and what was my problem? I reminded her of the time she had forsaken *me*. I actually used that word, *forsaken*, and it made her laugh. "I don't know what you're talking about," she said. "I was dealing with my dad that first summer back. He was a big mess by then so maybe I wasn't hanging out a lot with anyone. But I hardly ignored you."

My mother was away for a particularly long spell that year, visiting her parents. So I suppose it wasn't only the feeling of being rejected by Miriam that had put me in this state of mind. Whatever the cause, for much of that time I was overwhelmed by complicated emotions and an accompanying sensation of being pulled downwards. I realize this all sounds a bit airy-fairy. Let me share an incident that might better help illustrate my emotional state.

I remember it vividly, as though I'm looking through a series of colour photographs or watching a Super 8 film. It was the summer of Miriam's first return and I was standing outside jamat khana, evening prayers having finished. The sun was still shining, even though it must have been around eight p.m. The heat from the day had become less oppressive, and I could see that my father was in no rush to go home. He had just lit a cigarette and was talking with a group of men, his right foot resting on the fender of someone's car. A few women were standing apart from the men, in deep conversation. I stared closely at one of the women. The end of her chiffon sari floated off the small of her back as the wind gently lifted it up and set it back down. Multiple small groups of people were standing near them, talking, laughing, seemingly headed nowhere, giving the impression that this was a public square rather than a nondescript parking lot. I used to think of this particular lot as the front parking lot because it led to the only entrance to jamat khana. But the fact is, there was no actual front to this building. It was an old warehouse that, in the early 1970s, a group of Ismaili immigrants had repurposed into a house of worship. Warehouses are built for utility, to be on the back end, not the front.

Years later, in the months after Miriam died, I visited the jamat khanas our families had left behind in East Africa—in Mombasa and Dar es Salaam, in Kampala and Nairobi and Zanzibar, in Fort Portal and Masaka and finally in Mbarara. These were magnificent buildings, architectural masterpieces built with white stone and imported marble. The entrances were marked by wide steps and decorated columns. Clock towers reached into the sky. Some of these jamat khanas were surrounded by manicured gardens while others had massive ornate doors. All of them were works of art, designed to be admired, built to be seen.

But here, on Courtland Avenue in Kitchener, when I was eleven, jamat khana was hidden and practical and, if I am to think about it now, ugly. But I didn't think it ugly then. The truth is, I liked our jamat khana. I liked climbing up the narrow, grated, metal steps and through the heavy front door as though I were entering a secret passageway. The door led to a vast windowless room littered with hundreds of pairs of worshippers' shoes.

Once, my mother, my brother, and I had arrived to jamat khana late, my father working into the evening at the garage. As I bent down to remove my shoes, Saif mischievously kicked off one of his loafers, sending it soaring into the air so high it hit a tile in the drop ceiling. In a moment both the shoe and the tile came tumbling down. He stood with his mouth gaping, staring at the hole above him. I looked up as well, expecting to see the bottom of the carpets that lined the prayer hall and the people sitting on them fall through. But nothing more fell. My mother was enraged and expressed her anger as she usually did in a public place, by promising—through profane-laden whispers in Punjabi—a future punishment, which wouldn't come. She propped up the tile against the wall, straightened his shoes and quickly led us up the narrow stairwell.

Upstairs my brother walked into the men's side of the prayer hall. Before my mother and I went into the women's side we stopped in the women's coat room, which was actually multiple rooms, and which years later—long after the jamat khana on Courtland Avenue was shuttered—I thought of as the zenana. In my childhood, I didn't know what a zenana was. It was only after I had read about these South Asian women-only quarters in university and then later saw some on my backpacking trip through India, that I realized the women's coat room was in many respects exactly this: a space safe from even the possibility of men. Right now, as I imagine being in those rooms, I feel comforted. The men didn't have a coat room in our cavernous jamat khana. They would leave their coats on low shelves in the downstairs shoe room, off which was the men's tiny washroom. The zenana, on the other hand, consisted of a sprawling carpeted room with well-worn sofas; a washroom with multiple stalls and mirrors, which is where my mother would go to adjust her sari when we arrived; and another room with racks where coats hung. While she stood in front of the mirror, I would wander through the coats, disappearing in the darkness and the warmth and the scents of perfume and Indian hair oil and fried onions. But today there were no coats. Today it was midsummer and I was standing outside in the front parking lot.

I had been talking with a group of children, who over a period of a few minutes dispersed and disappeared. Some went home and others decided to walk to the convenience store nearby. I didn't want to go to the store, or maybe I thought they didn't want me to come along. I can't recall. It's very likely Miriam had been at jamat khana earlier that evening. But I have no recollection of seeing her on this occasion. The point is, I was standing alone and aimlessly. And then I noticed that a little boy had lingered behind with me. I knew him and his family. He was a sweet child, small for his age—which was five or six—and half my size. I looked around and saw that no one was watching us.

"Do you want to see something cool?" I asked him.

"What?" he asked, his eyes wide.

"It's not a thing. It's something really cool I can do. Promise," I said, "you'll be amazed."

He followed me to what I called the back parking lot, the one at the side of the warehouse, where no entrance to the building existed and where spillover cars parked on the big holidays when jamat khana was overflowing with people, but which today sat empty.

I wanted to get this boy alone so I could hurt him. This isn't accurate. I didn't want to hurt him in the sense that he would suffer. I wasn't thinking about his suffering or not suffering. He was a nice boy and I had no ill feeling towards him. I wasn't thinking about him at all. I wasn't thinking. I was responding to an urge so overpowering it was a physical ache deep in my solar plexus. I had the need to toss around someone small and vulnerable as though he or she (it didn't matter which) were a cartoon character, like Tweety Bird. It wasn't about this particular boy. He was merely an opportunity that presented itself to me.

He followed me until we reached a small patch of grass hidden behind rows of abandoned cars. I had pictured this moment, fantasized about it: throwing someone small and vulnerable and not quite real into the air, onto the ground. But as he walked with me, I became tired and disoriented, as though I were waking up from a dream. I told him to stand in front of me, with his back to me. He did as I asked. I stared at the top of his head, his black hair slightly oily and parted on the left side. He smelled like talcum powder; he smelled like a baby. The urge was completely gone. But he was waiting. And I had promised. I lifted him up by the waist, surprised by how heavy he was. I twirled him around once, maybe twice, weakly, and then set him down.

"That's it?" he asked.

But I had already begun to walk back to the front lot. I think he followed for a while, but I didn't look back. I went and stood by my father's car until he was ready to go home.

This is what I mean. I was in a strange emotional state in those days.

I wanted so badly to talk to Miriam about the experience with the little boy and what I had been feeling beforehand. But it was as though I no longer mattered to her. The problem was that she mattered to me. At jamat khana—the only place I saw her in those days—her attention was always on others, a group of others, who surrounded her everywhere she went. They would be laughing, and she would be performing. The centre of a storm that moved and shifted away from me as I stood quietly. Like a ghost.

Once, emboldened by my desperation to talk to her, I asked her if she wanted a cough drop. For half of fifth grade and the whole of sixth, I had repeating bouts of tonsillitis. On this day my mother had given me a pack of cherry-flavoured Halls, and I knew Miriam liked them.

"Sure," she said, "I'll take one."

I was thrilled to be acknowledged by her, but she was already walking away. She held out her hands behind her, palms open and outstretched, and continued walking. I sped towards her, trying to pull a cough drop out of the package while walking quickly. Awkwardly, I placed it in her hand.

"Thanks," she said without turning around or stopping. Then she was gone.

Miriam, with her new life in a new city, had become bolder, and she had always been bold. In the front parking lot, I heard her call her father "Dad," like a Canadian kid. She had begun to call herself *Mariam*, with a long "a" so that it sounded more like Mary. My father was still Papa. I knew most Canadians couldn't pronounce the phonemes in my name and that my mother would be devastated if I deliberately mispronounced it to accommodate them, so I avoided saying my name aloud, even to myself. Miriam had always announced herself loudly, in her rapidly acquired Canadian English, whether people wanted to listen to her or not.

A little more than a year earlier, before she'd moved to Burnaby, Miriam had joined my family for a picnic at Waterloo Park. After lunch, she and I wandered off. I was looking forward to walking on the wooded path, but Miriam veered away from me and walked up to a group of teenagers who were sitting at a picnic table drinking from poorly concealed beer bottles. She started talking to them as though she knew them, and as though they were her peers and not six or eight significant years older. They stared at her, raised their eyebrows, rolled their eyes, and then resumed talking among themselves. But Miriam was undeterred. She asked them questions. Inviting, flattering questions. Questions they seemed compelled to answer. "Your eyes are really pretty. Where did you get that eye liner? Is that a perm or natural hair? I wish I had hair like that. Is that a real tattoo? It's so cool." In the midst of the back and forth one of them said something outlandish, I can't recall what, and Miriam chanted, "Liar, liar, pants on fire," and they turned away, reminded all of sudden and again that this interloper was a child. But she wasn't finished. "Stick your ass on a telephone wire." She said the word "ass" triumphantly. And it was a triumph. They laughed, looked at each other, and then at her. They settled into the palm of her hand. She riffed; she told crude jokes; she referenced things I had never even heard of, things an eleven-year-old child should not know. I watched silently, aching to take part. But my mind moved too slowly. The teenagers didn't notice me. None of them looked in my direction. Miriam was a small kid; a little girl wearing white shorts with red piping, out of which stretched skinny, tawny legs. But she was bigger than this frame, she was more than this body. I was less. I was a shadow.

Thinking about it now, when Miriam and I were around other people, even when we were the best of friends, I often felt that she was alone on a stage. In those moments, not only others' but my own attention was fixed on her so completely that I disappeared. I don't mean this in a metaphorical sense. I really did— from my perspective—cease to exist, and yet of course I was there, living and breathing. I know this sounds completely contradictory. The best comparison I can think of is when you are in the city at nighttime and look up at the sky. The stars, obscured by the bright lights below, are invisible, though they have not, in fact, evaporated. Years later, Miriam explained this phenomenon. "It's caused by light pollution," she said. Light pollution was the reason she hated living in Toronto, she told me, and the reason she had to leave her husband and their downtown apartment. She explained that it was the city. The city was killing her. "Artificial, misdirected light," she said. "It obscures the light of the universe, the light of God." This was one of the rare instances when Miriam, who was an avowed agnostic, invoked God as something real. Of course, during this ethereal discussion she failed to mention the man for whom she was leaving her husband, the one who lived in the house in the country with its access to the stars and to God. But now I have veered far from what I wanted to talk about. Let me return to that summer, the one when Miriam and I were disconnected.

That July, as every July, my family attended the Kitchener Jamat Variety Program. This was an amateur show in which anyone in jamat khana—child, adult, even senior citizen—was welcome to perform, no audition necessary. The performances consisted of dancing, singing, short skits, and some Urdu poetry. In later years these variety shows were held in nice auditoriums, with seating and a stage with curtains. But back then the show was held down the street from jamat khana, in Courtland Public School's gymnasium. Although Miriam lived in Burnaby now, she remained a part of the Kitchener jamat—through her father and by virtue of the years she had spent here—and so took part in the Kitchener show, as she had always done. I, painfully shy and firm in my conviction that I had no talents to share, did not take part, that year or any other.

After the Gujarati folk dance and the Mohammed Rafi solo, after the Hindi film tribute, Miriam and a group of girls stepped onto the stage dancing to a disco song, a popular one that was constantly on the radio—"Funky Town" or "Le Freak" or something that Saif made fun of because he hated disco. It doesn't matter which exact song it was. The important thing to know is it was an English song. No one in the history of the variety program, to my knowledge, had ever performed to English music. All of the girls except Miriam were dressed in shiny, sparkly dresses or skirts. Most of them were not dancing so much as self-consciously swaying, and all of them were giggling. Miriam, wearing a crisp white dress shirt and black velvet pants, was neither giggling nor self-conscious. She was moving her body unabashedly, seemingly unaware of an audience or that her fellow performers weren't all that committed to this performance. At one point the group formed two lines and the dancers took turns strutting to the front of the stage between their fellow dancers.

It was noisy in the gymnasium. Small children were running around. Babies were crying. People were talking loudly in an effort to be heard above the din. But I was fixated on Miriam. She was at the centre of the stage, the centre of the performance, moving forward as she danced through the two lines of people. Suddenly she dipped to the ground and placed one hand on the floor behind her while kicking a leg forward. The dancers on stage clapped and hollered and a few people in the audience whistled. And then it was her turn to fall back, someone else's turn for the spotlight. But my eyes remained on her.

The next morning, I told my mother about Miriam and the other girls and the disco song. She was at my grandparents' house all the way in England and so I had to give her an update over the telephone. As I described the scene, I became more and more indignant.

"The song was awful," I said. "The whole thing was wrong."

My mother expressed some dismay, tepidly I thought, and started talking about something else. Pretty soon I brought up the variety program again, describing the beautiful Gujarati folk dance the older ladies did.

"This is a cultural show for our culture," she said.

I supposed this to mean Indian and also African and said so.

"Yes, of course," she said. "They should allow nothing else. Who even allowed this disco dance?"

"I don't know but they should be fired from the variety program committee," I said, shaking my head, even though of course she couldn't see me over the telephone. I went on and on about it, exaggerating things so that by my account the girls had been wearing super short skirts and heavy makeup, even though I could tell by mother's silence that she wasn't all that interested. At some point I stopped, not because I wanted to but because she reminded me this was a very expensive call and she wanted to hear about other things.

Later, at night, when I was lying in bed and thinking about the day, I was confused by my anger and by the pleasure I had taken in tearing down the dance and the girls. The truth is, as I had watched, I had been enthralled by the performance, by Miriam's performance specifically. I thought it was really good. What enraged me—I am seeing this only now—was that she was on stage and I was not.

Chapter 7

I SHOULD MENTION THAT in childhood I had other friends besides Miriam. Even when she lived in Kitchener, we both had our own social lives away from each other. We had a sixteen-month age gap, after all, and were two years apart in school.

I met a couple of Miriam's friends once, when I was arriving at Banting Place and they were leaving. Miriam introduced me by simply stating my name, which led me to believe she had told them of me prior to this meeting. She introduced them to me, on the other hand, as her "school friends." Come to think of it, whenever she spoke of other friends, she never referred to them as simply *friends*; they were only ever *school friends*. I didn't make this distinction with my friends. One girl, Jenny, was for a time during my childhood my best friend. Over the span of my life, it's fair to say Miriam was my closest friend, indeed my best friend. But during my childhood I had other best friends. They came and went. I think that's fairly typical, isn't it, especially for girls?

One fleeting friend in particular comes to mind. Her name was Beth and the last time I saw her, she was standing outside our high school smoking a cigarette. We were in the tenth grade and I remember thinking when I saw her: *Women shouldn't smoke.* This was for me at that time an unshakeable edict, one of those life rules that comes suddenly and forcefully to mind. I can't identify a moment in time or place when anyone stated this aloud. But I knew that my mother believed it. And, so, I believed it. Women shouldn't speak loudly or have sex before marriage or state their opinions unless asked or make financial decisions without their husband's or father's approval. These were life rules. I don't know when exactly they were imparted to me, just as I don't know when I had learned other simple edicts, such as to look both ways before crossing the road or to say thank you when someone gives you a gift or to close the screen door so mosquitoes don't come in.

"If you start smoking, I will kill myself."

I remember precisely the moment my mother said these words. It was that same summer when I was eleven and Miriam was ignoring me. One evening, shortly before my mother left for the UK to see her parents, she and I were lying on her bed. We had earlier witnessed some teenagers, one of them a fifteen-year-old girl from jamat khana. She was wearing faux-leather high-heeled boots, skin-tight jeans, and a tube top, and she was standing near the tire swing at Mackenzie King Public School, my school, with a white girl and a white boy, blowing cigarette smoke upwards into the cloudless sky. The tire swing had once been my favourite apparatus at that playground. But recently Jenny had taken to standing while I sat on it and using her legs to propel the swing with such force for so long—despite my pleas to stop—that my stomach lurched and I would be forced to walk home where I remained nauseated for the rest of the day.

I have no recollection of ever being at my school playground with my mother. But the image of the smoking girl remains a vivid tableau in my mind, the white teenagers framing the brown one. Looking back, perhaps my mother wasn't with me at all and I only related what I had seen. Nevertheless, the image prompted these words from her, words that settled on my chest like a whole other person, like Saif when he would wrestle me to the ground. I stared at my mother. She was lying on her back, her eyes closed and her arm resting over her forehead. Her lips were pursed slightly and moving, not trembling but almost, as though she were lost in a dream.

I looked away and pictured my father's Rothmans, always within his reach, on the side table, on the kitchen table, in the front pocket of his work overalls.

My mother placed an ashtray in every room of our house—even the bathroom—for him. They were pretty ashtrays made of clay and sometimes of glass, always in tones of orange or brown or green. One day she watched as I handed my father a clay ashtray I had made for him in art class. I had painted it bright orange.

Though she smiled when I proudly gave it to him, I know she thought my orange clay ashtray was ugly. She didn't say this, but she didn't display it anywhere in the house either.

Jenny, in those days, was trying lipstick, trying swear words, trying to make boys look at her, and she wanted to try smoking.

"Women don't smoke," I said.

She turned to me and laughed. "My mom smokes."

I stared at the ground.

"I guess she's not a woman, then," Jenny added.

I was quiet as she walked ahead of me up the hill towards the Catholic school. "I will never smoke. Ever." I said this after some time—maybe even as much as a minute—had passed. I said it so softly and she was so far ahead of me by then, she couldn't have heard.

I don't think Jenny was angry with me, because later we were at the playground at Mackenzie King Public School, racing on the wooden bridge that connected the treehouse to the monkey bars. I promised to go on the tire swing later, though I wasn't at all sure this was something I wanted to do. As we sat on top of the monkey bars, a schoolmate of ours—Beth—walked towards us. She joined us as children tend to do, without an invitation, and we all sat atop the bars and talked about the kids we hoped would be in our class in the fall, when we entered sixth grade, and the kids we hoped would not. Beth said she didn't really mind who was in her class but she seemed genuinely interested to hear our thoughts. As I watched Jenny talking and Beth listening, it occurred to me—to my surprise—that I liked Beth, that she was someone with whom I wanted to be friends.

Beth lived across the street from me. And for a time, a few years earlier, we had been good friends.

When my family first moved into our house five years earlier, Beth's house, and all the houses on that side of the street, hadn't existed. In their place was a wooded area that children at my school referred to as the bush. This was a relatively new suburb of Kitchener, built in the late 1960s, and the architecture of the houses—aluminum siding, split levels, attached garages, etc.—reflected this. But at the corner of the street, on the edge of the bush, stood an abandoned, two-and-a-half-storey brick house that clearly predated the rest of the neighbourhood. It had a wraparound porch, shutters that closed or were capable of closing, and a tall chimney. It must have been the house on a farm that once spanned this area. But to my six-year-old eyes it had no past; it was simply mysterious and terrifying. Convinced it was the home of witches—who only ever appeared at night because I had never seen anyone come or go from that property—I was careful never to walk on the same side of the street lest the inhabitants inside spy me.

Not long after we moved into the neighbourhood, someone set fire to the witches' house. It was a small fire and caused only smoke damage. A day or two later Saif told me that a boy in his class had been the arsonist. I shared this information with my teacher during reading time.

"I made that up!" Saif hollered when I told him I had confessed. "I was only telling stories. Why would you tell your teacher?" In the end my teacher must not have believed me since nothing came of it, no follow-up questions, not even any schoolyard gossip. A few months later, the witches' house was torn down.

By the time I was in the second grade, the bush in front of my house was razed and quickly replaced by a row of semi-detached houses. It was into one of those houses that Beth moved. She wasn't a new girl. Beth was already in my class at school. It occurs to me now that I never considered where she lived prior to moving to my street. It must have been nearby; no one was bused to Mackenzie King Public School. The truth is, I had never paid much attention to Beth.

On the day she and her family moved in, I watched them from my living room window. Beth, a purple sun hat on her head, was running around the yard holding a stuffed toy while adults carried boxes out of a big moving truck and through the front door. I don't know if it was because she was wearing that pretty purple hat or because I observed her at an exciting moment in her life, but Beth suddenly acquired a value she had not hitherto possessed. I walked outside and stood on my front lawn until she saw me.

Beth and I spent a lot of time together that summer, the summer after grade two. I played with her Barbie dolls and we listened to "Dancing Queen" again and again on her white turntable. Her house was smaller than ours but it was pristine. None of the walls had cracks or spots where the paint had faded. Beth's bedroom, bright with wall-to-wall carpeting, was packed with toys I had only dreamed of owning. I have no memory of Beth being inside my house, though I know we jumped rope together on my driveway. In any case, our friendship didn't survive the third grade. At school she no longer seemed interesting to me. I didn't understand why I became bored with Beth and I have no recollection of ending our friendship in any direct way, for example by telling her I didn't want to be friends, but the eventual outcome was that we stopped spending time together.

Not long afterwards, Jenny and I became best friends. We spent so much time exclusively with each other at school—in class and on the playground—that one day a teacher, watching us take turns at the water fountain, called us the Bobbsey Twins. I had never heard of the Bobbsey Twins, but I knew what twins were and I was thrilled that the teacher could see the similarities, rather than the differences, between a blue-eyed white girl and a brown-eyed Indian one.

As Jenny, Beth, and I hung out in the playground that day, two boys rode up on their bicycles. They dismounted, walked over, and stood next to the monkey bars. I knew the boys—they were in our grade—and had no reason to dislike them. But I was enjoying talking with the girls and felt some irritation at the intruders. I pretended they weren't there. Beth was looking at me as I continued to speak, but Jenny's attention was lost. She was stealing glances at the boys, preening in that way she had begun to do lately, throwing her head back and running her fingers through her hair like those women on the television commercials for shampoo.

"Why don't you guys come down?" one of the boys said. His name was Ted.

Jenny immediately climbed down. Beth followed and though I would have preferred not to, I felt I had no choice but to join them. The five of us sat in the shade next to the tire swing and talked about the summer we were enjoying when, apropos of nothing, Ted suggested we play a game called Spin the Bottle.

"It's a kissing game," he explained when we looked at him blankly. "You spin the bottle on the ground and wherever it points," he explained while demonstrating with an empty Coke bottle that had suddenly material-ized, "you have to kiss that girl. If you're a boy. Or the other way around: You have to kiss the boy if you're a girl. Obviously."

Jenny enthusiastically agreed to play. I didn't have any interest in kissing boys. The more I thought about kissing these two the more repulsed I felt. But I didn't want to be openly disagreeable and so I slowly inched backwards until I was out of the shade and sitting in the direct sunlight. My attempt to quietly disappear failed and the boys stared at me. I shook my head.

They turned to Beth, who shrugged. "Sure."

As I watched the four of them play Spin the Bottle, it became clear to me that the objective of this game for those two boys was to kiss Beth as much as possible. Neither Jenny nor I had developed any signs of breasts yet. In fact, if not for our long hair, we could easily have been mistaken for boys. Beth's body had a shape like a woman, with full, round breasts, a narrow waist, and a wide bum.

Each time Jenny had a turn to kiss or be kissed she did strange things, such as overly arching her lower back and letting her head fall back, so that Ted, in particular, told her repeatedly and with increasing impatience to relax. Then he began instructing her. "Move like this. Turn your head that way. No, that way."

In general, Jenny did not like being told what to do. During this game, however, she appeared to welcome whatever constructive criticism came her way. But it only served to make her more self-conscious than she already was so that now her movements were bordering on comical as she turned her head to one side, then the other, up, then down at Ted's frequent commands.

Beth was different. It wasn't merely that her body had developed much more quickly than Jenny's (and mine). It's that she was at ease. She didn't try at all. Whether it was climbing up the monkey bars or discussing school or kissing boys, Beth surrendered herself to it. As the game continued, I noticed the boys were spinning the bottle in such a way—say, moving it only a half-turn—to ensure that it pointed at Beth rather than Jenny. Eventually they were each simply taking turns kissing Beth. She let them climb on top of her and press their lips against hers as she lay on her back. She let them maintain mouth-to-mouth contact for a long time, as long as they wanted, and she seemed to know how to move her head and shift her body without any instruction whatsoever. Once, while Ted kissed her, she lifted her hand and gently held his head.

Later, when the streetlights came on and we all knew it was time to go home, the game ended. Ted patted Jenny on the shoulder. "Keep practising," he said. "You'll get it."

She smiled and heartily agreed, but as she turned away from him and towards me and Beth, she rolled her eyes. Beth, laughing, waved at us and left in the direction she had come, which was away from our houses. It didn't occur to me then to ask her why she wasn't going home. I recall watching her leave, her head tilted ever so slightly to one side as she walked, a habit I noticed when we were friends, a habit that echoed her mother's way of moving.

I've misremembered. It wasn't Jenny's mother who smoked, nor did we discuss it while walking towards the Catholic school. We were talking with Beth atop the monkey bars. And I had been staring at the tire swing.

"Women don't smoke," I had said in response to Jenny, who had declared she wanted to try.

"Of course they do," Jenny said. "Doesn't your mother smoke?" she asked, turning to Beth.

"Like a chimney," Beth replied.

"I guess your mom isn't a woman," Jenny said.

As they laughed, I recalled that my mother had said something else after she admonished me on pain of her death if I smoked: "Women who smoke are dirty and cheap."

I stared at the ground. When I looked up, I noticed that Beth had stopped laughing. She was smiling, kindly it seemed, at me. I smiled back and thought how much I liked her and wondered wistfully—almost painfully— why we weren't friends anymore.

"Come on!" Jenny hollered as she climbed down from the monkey bars and ran to the tire swing.

Beth followed.

I watched them, unable to move, until Beth turned and gestured with her hand for me to come. To join them. I did.

That's when the boys arrived.

* * *

I HAVE ONLY two other memories of Beth.

The first was three years later, a few days before the start of ninth grade, when I stood in my bedroom and watched from the window as Beth's father ran scream-ing down the middle of the road. I had been awoken by shouting, and I looked outside. I could see him under the streetlights, his gait unsteady, one arm reaching into the air as though he had been making a point in an argument and continued to do so even as he ran. He was slurring as he hollered, his words incomprehensible to me. A few metres ahead I saw Beth's brother—a young man who would have been twenty or twenty-one by then, running, not very quickly, but more steadily than his father. He was barefoot and wearing only a pair of jeans. Staring at the skin of his back, milky white against the night, I recalled Beth telling me years earlier that her big brother had dropped out of school.

"You can quit when you're sixteen," she had said as we sat on the floor of her bedroom. "And no one can stop you. Not even your parents." She seemed pleased as she shared this information with me. Proud of her brother or proud that she knew something I didn't. Or both.

I saw her that night, standing on the driveway with her mother, her hand over her mouth. Beth's mother ran after her husband and her son. "Stop!" I heard her scream. "Please!" But no one stopped. She jogged behind the man, who kept chasing his son, who was running farther and farther away until the night enveloped him. But Beth remained still. She glanced up at my window and I dropped to the ground, terrified she had caught me watching them, as though I had done something illicit. I huddled there as the shouting continued—another five minutes, or maybe just one. A door slammed. Then silence. I crawled into my bed without daring to look outside again.

The next afternoon, I saw Beth's father on his driveway washing his car, the radio blaring, as if nothing unusual had happened only hours earlier. And now and then over the next weeks I saw her brother, sitting on the porch smoking a cigarette, walking to the bus stop. I saw Beth too, leaving for school or maybe the mall, her eyes on the sidewalk in front of her, a white handbag with a long, thin strap hanging on her shoulder.

The last time I saw Beth was a little more than a year later, a few months before she quit high school. For some reason I cannot recall, I was walking out the back doors of the school, which opened onto the designated smoking area. Beth was standing alone, leaning against the wall, her blonde hair feathered and heavily sprayed so that it sat high on her head like a crown made of tissue paper. On a rainy day, years earlier, Beth and I had made paper crowns in her brightly painted bedroom. Her mother used her pinking shears to cut them for us, and I was amazed because my mother never let anyone use her sewing shears to cut paper. I wanted to remind Beth of the crowns we'd made, to share this sweet memory that had come to me all of a sudden. But she was staring straight ahead, away from me. A cigarette dangled between her first and second finger and smoke floated out of her mouth as she exhaled. She turned to me but the expression on her face registered nothing. It was as though she had no idea who I was. And, so, I kept walking.

Chapter 8

ETH IS THE friend I should have held onto. Not Jenny. Although I didn't hang on to Jenny. She clung to me. It might be more accurate to say she pulled me around. In fourth grade she loudly declared—first to me and then to others whenever the opportunity arose—that I was her best friend. She had this habit of grabbing me by the elbow and leading me wherever she wanted to go, to the tire swing, over to a gang of boys whose attention she wanted, to the back of the classroom.

Once, in fifth grade, my class did an assignment in which everyone wrote a letter to an unnamed advice columnist. Our letters were to remain anonymous and we had to be careful to avoid sharing any information that might give our identity away. When we handed them in, the teacher began to read each letter aloud and the class collectively offered advice. From the first letter, despite the teacher's protests, we tried to guess out loud whose letter it was. It was usually pretty hard to guess who wrote which letter. Until mine was read. I had described my frustration with a bossy friend who thinks she is better than me and demands I do only what she wants. Everyone, almost in unison, announced that this was my letter. Jenny didn't disagree but insisted—repeatedly—that it wasn't about her. No one believed her. Jenny had met Miriam one or two times, very briefly, and she knew Miriam and I were very close. I had not explicitly told her the letter was about Miriam, but I hadn't disabused her of the notion. To be clear, I had written the letter about Jenny. And I have to admit I was amused that the entire class knew this, while Jenny remained clueless. Despite this episode, however, we remained best friends.

One thing that kept us close was our love of sports. Jenny was a skilled ice skater. Each winter, her father built a rink in her backyard and encouraged her to play hockey with her older brothers. Skates, not to mention hockey equipment, were expensive. I struggled throughout my childhood in borrowed ill-fitting skates and came to hate skating. Jenny, in the meantime, became an excellent hockey player. I was better than her at softball. She was a good long-distance runner but, with my longer legs, I could beat her in a sprint. We were both competitive, but thankfully our different skill sets meant we rarely competed against each other.

One day, Jenny wasn't at school for some reason and a bunch of us were playing road hockey during recess. I was about to face off against Jeff, this boy in our grade who was, for those weeks, going with Jenny. This is how we described romantic relationships at my elementary school. A boy would ask a girl he liked: "Will you go with me?" And the girl would say yes or no. He wasn't asking her to go anywhere (indeed, no one actually did go anywhere as a couple as far as I'm aware); he was asking her to be his girlfriend. Some couples might have kissed (though I never witnessed this at my school). But mostly they walked around school together, either awkwardly side by side or, if they were particularly brave, hand in hand. As I was saying, when Jeff and I were about to face off, some people were discussing girls and sports and a comment was made about how good Jenny was at hockey. I agreed but added that I had beaten her once in a face-off, which I had. Once ice was removed from the equation, I could compete with anyone, including Jenny. Jeff immediately stopped the game and launched into a tirade about how beating someone once in a face-off means nothing. He explained to me, loudly, that beating Jenny once did not prove I was as good as her. For example, Jeff went on, he could "beat Gretzky one time." I was dubious but he was shouting. Still, I didn't argue with him. I was kind of in shock, not so much that a boy would come to his girlfriend's defence, but that he would come so hard for his girlfriend's best friend.

Come to think of it, being Jenny's best friend didn't keep me safe from her older brother, Tom, either. Whenever I encountered Tom—if his parents were out of earshot—he would hurl racial slurs at me. One afternoon, Jenny took me to an apple orchard near her house. I had no idea something like this existed anywhere, let alone walking distance from our neighbourhood. The trees were small and adorned with plump green apples, low enough for me to reach for one. I took a bite, and it was deliciously tart. I felt as though I'd stumbled into heaven.

Then Tom appeared and hollered for me to drop the apple. "Pakis don't get to eat these apples!" he screamed. I obeyed, more from the shock of him shouting than his reasoning. He kept on with the taunts—"No apples for Pakis!"—while I stood there, staring at the ground. Jenny told me to ignore him. But I couldn't. While he had called me Paki before, many times, he'd never so aggressively told me I couldn't do something. Tom was a year older than me and I was a bit afraid he might hurt me physically.

"It's okay," Jenny said. "Take an apple."

I shook my head; I must have looked as though I would cry or something because even the horrible Tom softened and told me to just have an apple. But I continued to shake my head. My refusal felt defiant. This defiance didn't erase the humiliation I felt, however, so it was hardly a victory. But even after Tom shrugged and walked away, I refused to touch another apple.

Other times, even years later, when Jenny and I were no longer friends, Tom would happen to be walking across the street as I headed home from school or to school, and he would holler in my direction. "Your house smells like shit and curry. Pakis smell like shit and curry!"

I looked Tom up online a few years ago. He looked terrible. He was extremely overweight and appeared decades older than his years. The comments under his photos on social media congratulated him for some weeks or months of sobriety. I probably should have had some compassion looking at this prematurely aged, sad man, now that we were both adults. But I felt none.

In the middle of sixth grade, Jenny found a new best friend. The two of them paired off in gym class and would whisper to one another and walk over to a secluded spot on the schoolyard during recess. If I wandered anywhere near them, they would run away from me, giggling. The new best friend telephoned me one afternoon and announced that Jenny hated me. It was a bit shocking, but at least it left no doubt in my mind that our friendship was over for good. But Jenny didn't leave it at that. More phone calls came. And the person on the other end (someone speaking in a low voice and talking of Jenny and the new best friend in the third person) addressed me as Munni.

Munni is a Gujarati term of endearment often used for little girls. It's nothing special or odd, but it was something my parents called me and had done since I was an infant. My mother still calls me Munni sometimes. Jenny knew this because she had visited my house a few times. I didn't really want people at school to know about things like my Gujarati nickname. I wanted them to think I was like them, that I ate the same foods and had the same history. I think this is a universal need children have: the desire to fit in. When Jenny would stay for dinner, I would beg my mother to make lasagna or fish and chips, which—because my mother worked in a factory and had limited time to create dishes that were for her pretty exotic—she refused to do. Most weekday evenings my mother would quickly whip up a simple chicken or beef curry, chapatis, and basmati rice. Jenny would be polite and say she loved it, but she would eat only a bite or two; I knew she hated it because normally she had a huge appetite. At my birthday parties we would order pizza and have popcorn and Coke and no one else at school—besides Jenny—knew that we ate weird things in our house.

During these telephone calls, someone speaking in the faux deep voice would say, "Hey Munni, where's your Mummy? Isn't it your bedtime?" or something like this. I would hear giggles and they would hang up. The calls would come when I was home alone, so I guessed someone was watching the house. It got to the point that I would jump when the phone rang. I remember rifling through the Yellow Pages trying to find out what to do if you are being harassed through the telephone. I even considered calling the police, but only for a few moments before dismissing the idea as silly. What I didn't consider was telling my parents. Nor did I tell Miriam. She was living in Burnaby and, in any case, she wasn't talking to me then. But the real reason I kept it to myself was because it felt like a shameful secret. No one else at school seemed to be aware this was happening. It was a secret bullying, now that I look back on it. I knew it would end eventually, so I did my best to absorb it quietly.

And then one day I was walking over to the Catholic school. It had a different playground than my school and sometimes on the weekend a few of my classmates would gather there. I don't recall who planned this particular get-together, but I recall that I expected people to be there. As I approached the playground, I saw that a sizeable crowd of my classmates, including Jenny, were indeed gathered, but they were all facing me and they were singing. I quickly ascertained that it was the song from the Dr Pepper soft drink commercial. Except they had inserted Munni in place of Pepper, so that they were singing, "I'm a Munni, you're a Munni, wouldn't you like to be a Munni too?" The words seemed to echo through the whole neighbourhood and I felt as though they weren't just making fun of me; they were making fun of my parents. I turned and walked home, tears streaming down my face.

Once again, I kept this to myself and said nothing to my parents about it. At school the following Monday no one spoke of it because a new drama had replaced it. A public health nurse had come to administer something called TB skin tests. Everyone in our class took turns having their inner forearms pricked. A few days later the nurse returned and checked our arms for any kind of reaction. My arm had a little pink welt where it had been pricked. As she walked around the class checking, it became clear to me no one else had such a mark. The nurse called me outside the classroom, where another nurse, who had set up a desk, was waiting. In the hallway they both looked at the welt.

"Where were you born?" one of them asked sweetly. "Uganda," I replied.

"Oh? Wasn't it India?" she said, as though I had made a mistake.

I shook my head. "My grandparents left India and moved to Uganda," I said. "And Idi Amin kicked Indians out, so we came to Canada as refugees." I had been asked the question of my birthplace many times by then and had a couple of standard phrases to explain why a South Asian girl was from an East African country. My family had spent a year living in Kenya before settling in Kitchener. But I generally left that part out to keep it simple. In any case, my answer seemed to clarify something for the nurse.

"This must be why you have this lovely colour," she said. She was staring at my arm, at the welt, when she said it and so I took this to mean the "lovely colour" of my welt, not my skin in general. I knew—because the nurse had explained this before administering the tests—that TB was short for tuberculosis, which was a terrible disease. And I refused to believe I had a terrible disease. But the nurse handed me an unsealed letter to give to my parents. It stated that I had tested positive for TB and needed further testing, including a chest X-ray. So, now, besides having no friends, I was dying.

The next morning I felt sick to my stomach, so my mother let me stay home from school. Later that day, I was lying on the carpet watching *The Price Is Right* when the show was interrupted by a special news report. A big group of Americans who had been held hostage in Iran had arrived home to the United States. It was a very happy occasion as families hugged and cried tears of relief and joy. It seemed in direct opposition to how I was feeling. I felt so sorry for myself in that moment that even the newly released hostages—who had been kept locked up for more than a year—were lucky compared to me.

Later that week I had a chest X-ray and visited our family doctor, who assured me I did not have tuberculosis. This doctor was a family friend who was also from Uganda. He explained that I, unlike my Canadian-born classmates, would have received a vaccination against tuberculosis when I was in school in Kenya. It's a live vaccine, he explained to my mother and me, and this is the reason I tested positive on the

TB skin test. My mother was able to produce—after a short search through my father's files—the immunization form in question. With this, my brush with mortality was over.

When Miriam arrived the following summer, she told me she too had a TB test and she too tested positive. This conversation actually marked the resumption of our friendship. I was outside jamat khana on a Friday evening, after prayers were finished, leaning against my dad's Oldsmobile trying to pull my hair back into a ponytail because it was so windy when Miriam walked up, seemingly from nowhere (I don't recall seeing her inside earlier). She nonchalantly asked me how I had found grade six.

"Did you like being at the top of the food chain?" she asked.

I told her that I hated the whole year, and also I had thought I was dying.

"Maybe there's something in us, you know?" she said, after we discussed the TB tests. "Something in our blood. That's why only you and me tested positive."

I knew this wasn't the case. I more or less understood how the vaccination had caused a positive result. Miriam should have understood this too, even better than I did because she was older and good at science. But it's as though she were being wilfully blind to the logical explanation. I think she liked believing we were somehow different, in a tangible way, from our classmates. I liked it too in that moment, and so I didn't challenge her. Instead, I told her about the taunting at the playground.

I expected Miriam to feel sorry for me, as I did, particularly as we had just bonded. But she laughed.

"They were singing about you," she said. "Why did you go home?"

"They were making fun of me," I said, indignantly.

"You could have said, 'Yeah! You're right! I'm Munni! A munni is a queen.' How would they know? What does it mean, sweetie or something? It's not a bad word. It's not a mean word."

"You know they meant it in a bad way," I said.

"Maybe. But I think you felt bad because they were shouting what you want to hide."

"What do I want to hide?" I asked.

"You," Miriam said. "You want to hide you."

Chapter 9

OVER THE NEXT year Miriam changed physically. She was thirteen now and had noticeable
curves. Her new figure wasn't anything
dramatic; she was a slight girl. But to me—who at
twelve was gangly, not yet menstruating, and still
sleeping with a large collection of stuffed animals—
she looked almost grown up. That summer was the
first time I became aware of how pretty Miriam was.
Although it's not really accurate to say I became aware
of it as much as I noticed others around me remarking
on it. My mother had started, for example, to comment
on her looks with regularity. It was always a statement
of surprise that simultaneously insulted her parents.
She would say, to Miriam's face, something along the
lines of: "How did Hassan and Begum make such a

beauty?" Or "I don't know where in the world you got these looks." After she said this type of thing to Miriam, my mother would look at me and smile—kind of pity-ingly, I thought.

At that age, I was oblivious to the reasons Miriam was considered pretty and I wasn't. It was also the year I took up playing basketball. Ever since my rapid growth spurt, when I met adults, either for the first time or after some passage of time, they would say—I suppose because they could think of nothing else to say to a tall girl—one of two things: "You should be a model" or "You should play basketball." I knew that I wasn't pretty, and so when the suggestion of modelling came up, I would try to become invisible (by turning away or looking down). I was afraid if they looked at me a moment longer, they would realize this was a ludicrous proposition and announce this painful fact, thereby embarrassing us both.

But the other suggestion turned out to be a good one. I enjoyed basketball. I felt when I was in a gym that I was allowed to play and be a child, in the sense of not feeling compelled to be ladylike or demure or, of course, pretty (attributes much valued by my mother). Miriam didn't like sports but she also didn't like makeup and using a curling iron on her hair or anything like that, at least not yet. So, her burgeoning beauty didn't affect our friendship in any substantial way.

A few years later, I would see what others saw in Miriam. She had a clear, olive complexion; delicate, symmetrical features; and stunning hazel eyes. Her face lit up when she smiled. I was large featured and dark-skinned, not a monster or anything like that. I was and am okay looking. But I knew that my appearance wouldn't give me an advantage in any way. Not like Miriam. She had the kind of beauty that would turn heads on the street and make boys or men stammer in her presence.

Miriam was probably in her mid-teens when she started to harness the power of her looks. She would tell me stories about making out with boys at her high school in Burnaby or of going on dates without Begum knowing. On these dates, the boys would pay for everything: movie tickets, popcorn, dinner even. One boy took her out on his father's sailboat.

I wasn't sure how to react to these stories. Miriam made it a point to relate how little she liked the boys in pretty much all instances. She accepted their invitations because, for example, she felt like seeing a particular movie or she thought the sailboat would be cool. I thought Miriam was cheapening herself, but this realization came to me years later. At the time I felt a slight discomfort and a lot of curiosity about what she was telling me.

The thing is, my mother believed—and taught me to believe—that the way you behaved gave boys and men an idea of your value. I spoke a bit about this earlier, when I told you how my mother used to insist that women should be submissive around men. If you were forward, you were seen as too easily acquired and would be treated as an inexpensive trinket might be. I realized it was like supply-and-demand economics. I remember saying this to Miriam once, when we were undergrads. We had been speaking over the phone about a crush I had on a professor.

Miriam was advising me to make my attraction and intentions clear. But I didn't agree because of the aforementioned issue of my value. I explained myself by sharing the supply-and-demand comparison. I felt pretty clever and also kind of triumphant because Miriam was quiet for a few moments after I said it.

"I guess," Miriam said, finally, "if you see yourself as a commodity."

"It's only a metaphor," I said. "It's not a perfect comparison. But you get my point."

"I get it," she said. "I just don't agree."

Somehow, we got to talking about my mother. I suspect I may have brought her up to defend my position because Miriam was commenting about our mothers' attitudes towards relationships in general.

"They're of a generation—and culture—that believes a woman can't exist without a husband or a father," Miriam was saying. "They weren't taught to view marriage as a partnership. For them it was a validation. Begum fought with everything she had to stay in her marriage, both marriages, even though she hated her husbands. For her, you are not a legitimate human being unless you belong to a man. Same for your mom. I mean, she stayed with your dad despite all his cheating."

I asked her to stop. This wasn't fair or accurate, at least not with respect to my mother. To prove my point, I shared something I had kept from Miriam for years. I'm not sure why I phrased it this way. I hadn't necessarily kept it from Miriam. I simply hadn't told her or anyone for reasons I will explain shortly.

This incident happened when I was eleven. It was that eventful year, if you recall, when Miriam ignored me, and my mother had been away a great deal. By the fall, my mother was home, Miriam was in Burnaby, I was back in school, and, as far as I was concerned, life was back to normal. One Saturday, I was lying on my parents' bed watching television when my mother walked in and sat down beside me. She sat stiffly: her back was upright and she was staring straight ahead at the mirror above her dresser rather than at me or at the television in the corner. "I need to talk to you about something," she said to her own reflection.

I didn't switch off the television or turn down the volume. In those days we didn't have remote controls and her request didn't seem serious enough to warrant my standing up and walking over to the television. Her behaviour was odd, certainly, but not terribly alarming and I was enjoying my Saturday morning cartoons. As I describe this scene, it's unclear to me why I wasn't in the basement. That's normally where I would watch television. My father would have been working at the garage, as he did every Saturday. I don't recall where Saif was. In any case, my mother said something to the effect of wanting me to know something "first." This intrigued me and I sat up and gave her my full attention, though I still didn't move to switch off the television or even to turn the volume down.

"I am divorcing Papa," she said and lowered her eyes. "I have found an apartment, but I won't move there quite yet. When I do, and after things settle down, you and Saif will come live with me." She offered no further explanation, including what she meant by "after things settle down," but now she turned to look at me.

"Why would you get an apartment?" I asked, almost spitting the words out. A terrifying picture had emerged in my mind of her standing inside a fully furnished apartment, refusing to let my father, Saif, and me inside, even as we begged and pleaded outside the locked door.

"For too many years," she said, "I've asked: Where will I go? What will I do? This isn't a reason to stay in a marriage." She took hold of me, gently, by the shoulders. "Do you understand? I need you to understand." She said this sweetly, the way she would when I was small and she was patiently explaining a game or something. But there was also a hint of desperation in her voice.

I didn't understand.

"I want you to know this," she said. "I am your mother and I am not going to leave you. It isn't possible to leave you and Saif because you are a part of me. But I need to leave him."

I didn't know what to say or do at this point. I remember turning towards the television and seeing the cartoon, a coyote blowing something up and managing to ignite himself as usual, and it seemed far away and uninteresting. I looked back at her and nodded. I felt very much that she wanted something from me and that's all I could give her.

She seemed pleased by my reaction and hugged me. "We will all talk about it, you, me, Papa, and Saif, a little later. But I wanted you to know before anyone." Then she walked out of the room and went downstairs.

In those days—it was the early 1980s—divorce seemed to be coming up a lot, in movies and on television shows, even in school. Once, a teacher asked how many students in the class had parents who were still married and I proudly raised my hand, almost intoxicated by the superiority I felt over a solid third of the class who kept their hands lowered. But now I could no longer be better than them. Now my family too would be fractured. As I sat alone in my parents' bedroom, I wanted to tell Miriam, but she was in Burnaby and in any case wasn't my friend any longer. When I saw my father later, and then Saif, I said nothing about what my mother had told me. I was waiting for her to begin the conversation. But she didn't. Days went by and still she said nothing.

About a week or maybe two weeks after our conversation, my father was diagnosed with cancer. It was found fairly early and it could be treated. He needed care and my mother provided it: nursing him after surgery, driving him to medical appointments and to pick up medication. Of course, she cooked whatever he needed or wanted and cleaned up after him, but she had always done that. And she did it all while keeping her job at the shirt factory. His full recovery from surgery and chemotherapy took about a year. My mother never again mentioned divorce or the apartment.

"I guess his cancer killed her momentum," Miriam said after I finished telling her this story.

"I don't know," I said.

"Do you think she realized she loved him and wanted to be married to him?" she asked. "After all?"

"Maybe," I said. "Maybe that's what it was. For so long, I wondered if I had dreamt that she talked to me about divorce. Like maybe it didn't happen. That's why I never said anything to you or anyone. She never said a word about it again. Not a word. But now that I'm recalling it, she wasn't the same. She couldn't hide how much she resented him anymore. She'd mutter under her breath and roll her eyes when he talked sometimes. When he died, she was sad but not about losing him. I think she was sad about how much of her own life she had lost.

"What I'm saying is you're right. The cancer killed the momentum she had built to finally leave. It knocked the wind out of her sails, and she was stuck."

"She was ready to live without him," Miriam said. "She went as far as to find an apartment. It's amazing. For someone like her, the way she was raised, it's amazing. She was right that you can be, or you should be, independent in a marriage. You shouldn't be in it because you have nowhere else to go. I think that's it. I think that should be the goal. A marriage of two independent people."

I agreed with Miriam completely. But then about ten years later, when I was moving in with my boyfriend, Miriam said something that flipped what we had talked about that day on its head.

My then boyfriend, Ben, was twelve years older than me and divorced. He wasn't keen to be married again. In fact, he told me it wasn't something he could see himself ever repeating. His divorce had been painful, and I didn't think it fair to insist I wanted to be married if it troubled him so much. But at the same time, I felt as though I were being cheated. I told Miriam that it was totally okay because I didn't want the "label of wife anyways." She seemed to admire this. I don't know why I lied to her. I suppose I was ashamed. Ben was a good man and I really did love him, and I believed he loved me too. But he had a wife. They were divorced and had been for quite a few years before he and I met, but when the word "wife" came up, on television, among friends—just incidentally I mean—I pictured her, and I'm sure he did as well. He married her and wore a ring for her and committed himself to her legally. Things he wouldn't do for me.

My mother was surprisingly okay with us living together unmarried. I think she was happy I wasn't alone anymore, as she told me. But she did insist on throwing us a party during which she could carry out a few Indian ceremonies, the ones done when a girl leaves her parents' house and joins her husband's family. I didn't see the harm in this and submitted to vermillion being placed on my forehead and rice being tossed around us. Ben was fascinated by it all and, in the end, it turned out to be a lovely party. Miriam even flew in for it. She came straight from the airport and I immediately noticed she seemed a bit intoxicated. Her eyes had that glassy look they got when she had been drinking. After eating some dinner, she had a strong drink—a martini—so when she asked everyone to be quiet to allow her to say a few words, I was nervous. I considered for a moment trying to talk her out of it, but it all happened so fast and there she was, standing in front of the fireplace in Ben's living room, all eyes on her. It was silly, I suppose, to be nervous of what she'd say. But thinking back, I was afraid she'd talk about Ben refusing to marry me and how she was here to convince him. Or something equally embarrassing. But she didn't say anything like that. She talked about science.

"There's this phenomenon, in physics," she began, "called a quantum entanglement. I promise I won't bore you with things that remind you of high school science, if you will just bear with me. Let's say," she said in that peculiar—patient, indulgent even—tone she took on when she was determined to make me understand a complex physics concept, "you have a pair of quantum objects—I'll call them quantum friends. In physics we say the friends in the pair are independent if knowing something about one of the friends doesn't reveal anything about the other. On the other hand, we say a pair of friends is entangled when information about one improves our knowledge about the other. Like how if you find the left hand of a pair of gloves, you know the missing one is the right hand.

"There are many ways to create entangled objects, or I should say, friends. One way is to place them together and let them interact in such a way that the final states of the two particles depend on each other. Essentially, the pair will come to exist together in a state of quantum superposition, which means—" and here Miriam pointed at me.

"It means they are in a state of potential, a wave and a particle, both at the same time," I said, having been well coached by her over the years, "until observed."

"Exactly," she said, "or, like Schrödinger's cat in a box, simultaneously dead and alive until observed. So that unlike the pair of gloves, which are fixed objects, these entangled friends have not collapsed into a thing; they are simply the possibility of becoming something. But," she said, raising a finger in the air, "they are linked so that when they do collapse, they do so in the same moment, no matter how far apart they are. The behaviour of one is inextricably linked to the behaviour of the other. If one is spinning one way, the other is spinning the opposite. If one is up, the other will be down. Our friends remain connected even if they are on opposite ends of the galaxy, even if they are separated by billions of light years."

There was at this point some murmuring of approval.

"Nothing can disentangle them," Miriam said, pausing for effect. "Nothing. Not distance, not time, not death." She held up her glass towards me and Ben. "This is my wish for you. Entanglement. For eternity."

It's odd, isn't it? That she would make such a speech when she didn't believe this? When she believed the opposite, that independence in relationship was, as she herself said, the goal. Certainly, I was grateful she made the speech. Miriam didn't appreciate it when I took scientific concepts and turned them into metaphors, and so I accepted this speech as a gift, a pretty generous gift. But my intention in sharing it with you was to demonstrate how Miriam said one thing but believed another. And yet as I describe the moment when she held up her glass, I realize something. Miriam wasn't looking at Ben and me; she was looking only at me. Her speech wasn't about a romantic couple at all. It was about us: Miriam and me. It was about our entanglement.

Chapter 10

WHEN I MENTIONED earlier that I had a crush on a professor it reminded me how Miriam and I had a tendency to fall for our instructors at university. I don't think this is all that unusual, is it? Maybe you too admired a professor at some point or, at the very least, knew someone who did. But with us it did seem to happen a lot. I think it's because we didn't know anyone, personally, who had gone to university. And, so, people with PhDs seemed like movie stars or something, unattainable and otherworldly. At least it was this way for me. Miriam was attracted to profs too, of course, but she believed the stars in her life—to continue the metaphor—were within her reach.

During my first year at the University of Toronto, for example, I became infatuated with my middle-aged

Latin professor. I would send Miriam long letters describing the looks I imagined he was giving me or funny things he said or clues I discovered that revealed he was unmarried and thus available. Miriam wrote back, rather more briefly, about a teaching assistant who she said was flirting with her. I should point out here that Miriam and I exchanged a lot of letters throughout the years. Sometimes we would talk over the phone, but this was rare. During her undergrad she was across the country at the University of British Columbia and long-distance calls were expensive then. What this meant with respect to my crushes is that my drama-filled letters to Miriam gave my romantic dreaming a tangible quality. Because while this thing I had with my Latin professor felt real in the sense that my feelings were intense, I don't think I had one conversation outside class with him. Our romantic interactions—or hints of them, I should say—existed entirely in my head.

This was not the case with Miriam. After Christmas break that year, she called me up to wish me a happy new year and told me that over the holidays she had started sleeping with Andrew, the teaching assistant. I was stunned. For one thing, I was still a virgin and Miriam said "sleeping with" like it was no big deal. But also I didn't actually believe it. Imagine if you and your friend enjoy talking about a couple of characters, let's say on a soap opera, and then one day your friend calls you up and announces that she is now having sex with one of them. Would you believe it? I told her she must be putting me on. She was quiet. I thought for a moment that she had hung up on me. Then a man came on the line and, laughing, introduced himself as Andrew.

They were together a short time, in the end. Only about six months. Miriam lost her virginity to him. She told me this about a year later. At the time she was with him I had assumed, because of the way she casually described sleeping with Andrew, that she must have had sex earlier, maybe with one of the boys she dated in high school. The reason I didn't clarify this with her is that whenever I broached the subject—for example, once I asked, "How do you manage, you know, doing it, with your roommate always in the dorm?"—she was dismissive and changed the subject.

Another time, in response to my fishing for information about her sex life, she seemed downright irritated with me. "Everyone has sex. It's normal and not a big deal. If you treat it like it's a big deal, you'll turn guys off."

For as long as I can recall my mother would casually bring up the fact that she had not kissed my father (or any man) before she married him. Whatever we were talking about—characters in a movie, the bride and groom at the wedding we were attending, my future life as someone's wife—my mother would share, in more or less these words and in this order, the following two statements: 1. "He says we kissed before marriage but we never did." 2. "I didn't know anything at all. I was such an idiot."

As I share this now, I'm a bit shocked. Not by what she said; this is a familiar refrain from my childhood and adolescence. What shocks me is that I always focused on the first statement rather than the second. I had assumed forever that my mother was immensely proud of being a chaste bride. But looking back now, the word "idiot" stands out. What she actually said in Punjabi is budhu, which pretty much means "idiot," maybe "fool" in its most charitable translation. In any case, what I am trying to point out is that I used to aspire to be like my mother, or at least what I believed her to be. To that end, I spent my teen years expecting to wait to have sex if not until I was married, certainly until I was in a committed relationship. (Holding off on kissing seemed a bit extreme.) But as my teen years were coming to an end, I had doubts that this was the best course. Even though I had not yet kissed a boy, I knew that many girls in high school had been sexually active; I had heard of at least two pregnancy scares in grade 13. That same year our guidance counsellor handed out condoms—this was at the height of the AIDS epidemic—and no one giggled. Everyone acted nonchalant about it, stuffing two or three condoms in their pockets. My roommate at university, the one assigned me by Trinity College and so not an actual friend of mine, was on the birth control pill. She was always freaking out that she had forgotten to take it. Although, looking back, I saw no actual signs of a boy or man in her life and so it's very likely she was prescribed the pill for her acne. The point is I started to believe I was, at nineteen and a virgin, a bit of a freak. I feared, as Miriam had warned, that this fact would get in the way of acquiring a boyfriend, which is something—I'm sure you can understand if you were ever a teenaged girl—I very much wanted.

One weekend around that time I had a bad episode of what I guessed was food poisoning and went to the university medical clinic. The doctor on duty was young and sufficiently attractive that I was a bit nervous discussing my diarrhea. While he was trying to rule out potential causes of my gastrointestinal problems, he asked me if I was sexually active. I don't know if it was my expression or the way I shook my head, but he suddenly became awkward. He folded his arms, leaned back on his heels, and said, really slowly, "So, you have never been sexually active?"

I stared at him.

"What I mean to say is, you've never had sex? Is that right?" He was a red-haired guy, or strawberry blonde I suppose would be more accurate, and when he asked this last question his face turned pink. I think before Miriam started talking about sleeping with Andrew I might have been proud about the fact I was a virgin. But now I felt ashamed to admit it. I did, in the end, admit it to him, if for no other reason than to ensure I wasn't subjected to some sort of embarrassing internal exam.

A few weeks later I had drunk sex with a boy from my introductory British literature class. Immediately afterwards I regretted it. Not because I wished I had remained a virgin (I didn't) but because the whole episode left me feeling a little bit sad.

What happened is a few people from our class had gone to a pub one evening. I drank tequila shots for the first time and felt euphoric and strangely powerful. In this state I invited the boy up to my room. On the way, in the hallway, we stopped and he leaned me against a wall and kissed me. He just shoved his tongue into my mouth. I was in equal parts stunned and repulsed, but I knew this was how it was done so I let him continue for a bit before leading him by the hand to my room. I should point out that I didn't actually like him (physically or otherwise), but desire was irrelevant in this circumstance. I wanted to get my virginity out of the way. We made out for a few more minutes inside my dorm, and then I assumed we would have sex on my bed and so lay down on my back and unbuttoned my shirt until my bra was just visible (as I'd seen women on television do), waiting for him to climb over me. But he stepped forward, grabbed hold of my forearms, and pulled me up to a standing position. Then he pushed me, not super hard but pretty firmly, against the wall so that for a moment I was frightened he would hurt me. Then he stepped back and said, not rudely but in a breathless, almost impatient voice, "Is it okay if we do it standing up? I think that might be easier for me."

I wasn't attracted to him, as I say, at all; I felt in fact as though I were playing a role, like an actor in a movie. So I went with it and said sure or okay or something like that, and we both dropped our jeans and got it over with. Well, not quite. First, he awkwardly unwrapped a condom and struggled to put it on for a bit while I stared at my roommate's organization calendar on the wall behind him. As you can imagine, it was uncomfortable and painful and made me feel lonely, even while he was literally inside me.

I avoided him in class after that, even though sometimes he would try to talk to me, to be polite, I guess. The thing is I had accomplished what I set out to do, but I felt badly about it. Try as I might to forget it, I couldn't. You know how when you've said something embarrassing at a party or in class and each time you recall it you close your eyes tightly, as though you can make the memory disappear, but that only seems to make it more vivid? It was like that. It's funny because although both of us were up front about what we wanted from each other, I felt cheated. As though he took more than he gave me in the transaction.

I'm reminded of something. An experience—though wildly different—that left me feeling the same way. This happened when I was much younger, in the fourth grade. It was the late 1970s and chestnut fighting was all the rage at my school. There were quite a lot of chestnut trees in my neighbourhood and in the fall, you could find the chestnuts scattered on the grass. I suppose some people picked them from the trees, but I never did. Any chestnuts I acquired were from searches along the ground. Once you found your chestnut, you would pierce it with a nail and then pull a shoelace through it, knotting it on one end so the chestnut didn't slip off. Then you and an opponent, likewise armed with a chestnut on a shoelace, would kneel in the dirt and hit each other's chestnuts by swinging the shoelace. I don't know what it was like at your school, but at ours we would dig a small, shallow hole in the dirt with our hands and that's where the chestnut fight would take place. There were loads of these holes around the schoolyard each fall. So after a few weeks you didn't need to dig them anymore, unless there had been a big rainfall.

Some people insisted there was artistry to the flicking and swinging. But I think it came down to the chestnut and how strong it was. People had all sorts of tricks to make their chestnuts strong. You could rub them with vinegar or vegetable oil or bake them or freeze them. Some people swore that keeping your chestnut under your pillow for a few weeks worked. The owners of the strongest chestnuts usually wouldn't share their secrets, for obvious reasons. I tried all the methods. Once, my mother let Saif and me put a couple of chestnuts in the oven when she was cooking something else. I think in the end the method that worked for me was forgetting about a chestnut I had placed in my sock drawer. I found it a whole year later and it was as hard as a pebble. It turned out to be a real weapon. I won fight after fight. When not playing, I hung the chestnut around my neck and felt pretty good about myself.

One Saturday afternoon I was at the school playground alone when I was approached by some boys from the sixth grade. They asked me about the chestnut I had hanging around my neck and how many times I'd won and what I'd done to make it so strong. One of them said he saw me playing softball and noticed I was a good hitter. He even knew my name. At one point the other guys drifted away and this guy stayed behind. After a few minutes of talking about softball he offered to trade me his chestnut for mine. He didn't lie or anything. He said mine was way better than his, but he admitted he felt like a loser and it would mean a lot to him to win sometimes.

"You're a smart girl. You get it. I mean, I'm a sixth grader. I can't be losing to little kids all the time." When he said this, he patted my shoulder and looked directly in my eyes.

I made the trade. He thanked me about ten times. I felt so good I had made him happy that I didn't care that I'd probably never win another chestnut fight again.

The following Monday, as expected, my new chestnut cracked within the first seconds of a fight. I saw the boy during afternoon recess. He didn't avoid me exactly. He smiled a little, almost sheepishly, and then he walked past me without saying anything. Over the next days I watched him win fight after fight. I also overhead people talking about his chestnut and how he had been working on it for ages to make it strong. I felt so stupid. And I hated the boy.

That's how I felt in my dorm after having sex. Both times I felt acutely sorry for myself, as though I'd been tricked. But now that I look back on it, I realize no one had promised me anything they didn't deliver. They asked for something and I gave it to them. If I valued my body or that chestnut, I had a poor way of showing it, didn't I? So, I suppose that's on me.

Let me get back to what I was telling you about Miriam and Andrew. She eventually told me in a letter—as I say, about a year after they split up—that he had been her first time. He took it slow and gentle, and he lit a bunch of candles and played a Leonard Cohen cassette to get her in the mood.

I was so angry after reading that, I ripped up her letter and vowed not to write or call her ever again.

Chapter 11

GOT OVER BEING annoyed with Miriam pretty quickly. I doubt she noticed my short-lived silent treatment. It was the end of term, and during exams she tended to keep to herself more than usual. The truth is, it was Miriam who would suddenly stop talking to me for a time, rather than the other way around. It wasn't that she was mad at me; she more or less stopped communicating with anyone. We came to call these silences her Lows. I can't remember exactly when we named them this. But after she had experienced a few of these quiet periods, I suggested what she was going through was depression. She said it wasn't quite that. What would happen, she explained, is that her energy would drop really low and her body felt actually—meaning literally—heavy so that she couldn't bring herself to do much, physically or mentally. But she wasn't thinking particularly sad or depressing thoughts. She wasn't thinking much at all. So it wasn't accurate, she said, to call it depression. One of us, I honestly don't remember who, called it the Lows. It stuck.

When Miriam was in her Lows, she wouldn't telephone me or write to me or answer my letters for a long time, about three months or so. Then one day she would call me to let me know she was in the Lows. She didn't want to talk much on those calls; she'd ask me to speak so she could listen. "Tell me what you're reading," she'd say, for example. And I'd go on a bit about whatever novel I was reading or the poem I was assigned. I remember once telling her how amazed I was to discover that John Keats created movement with words.

"So, the poet is sitting in a garden and he's very sick, he's dying of tuberculosis—but this isn't in the poem; I know this from the notes—and he is listening to a nightingale's song and it transports him from the agony of being in his body to the ecstasy of the birdsong. But this great feeling can't last, of course, and the nightingale flies away. The way he describes it, though, sounds like a bird flying," I said. "You need to read it pretty quickly to get the effect. 'Adieu! adieu! thy plaintive anthem fades,' and here it comes or, I guess, here it goes," I said:

Past the near meadows, over the still stream,
Up the hill-side; and now 'tis buried deep
In the next valley-glades.

When I finished Miriam didn't respond and I wondered if she was even on the phone. "Do you hear it?" I asked. "Do you hear how the words mimic the nightingale flying?"

"I hear it," she said.

I thought she was being polite or something because her voice sounded flat and she didn't offer any commentary at all. We ended the call not long after that. A couple of weeks later, a letter from Miriam arrived. In it, she wrote about how much she had fallen in love with "Ode to a Nightingale" and that she had been falling asleep at night repeating lines from it in her head.

She wrote out this bit in the letter:

My heart aches, and a drowsy numbness pains
My sense, as though of hemlock I had drunk,
Or emptied some dull opiate to the drains
One minute past, and Lethe-wards had sunk.

"When I read these words—with all the *p*'s and *m*'s—out loud," Miriam wrote, "my lips feel numb, like they're too big for my mouth, like when I'm drunk." Then she added, "You're right, what Keats does with words is amazing."

I was shocked. I didn't think she was even paying attention to me. And yet she had gone out (probably to the library), despite being in the Lows, and found the poem and written out parts of it.

I realize looking back that this experience, and a few others like it, led me to believe Miriam's Lows weren't that low, that she could come out of it pretty easily if I talked to her and maybe read her some good poetry, because the truth is, this usually did the trick.

I remember a conversation that Miriam and I had when we were both living in Toronto a few years later. We had gotten into the habit of meeting for breakfast twice a month or so, either at one of our dorms, where we would have a coffee and some pastries, or—if we had a bit of extra money—at a restaurant. On one of these occasions, we were at a restaurant near my graduate residence on Bloor at St. George, I asked her if the Lows are what led to her interest in dark matter.

"Dark matter isn't particularly ominous or dark in the sense we think of it," she explained. And then she added, in a flippant tone, "You and your metaphors."

"Isn't it called dark because it's unknown?" I asked, with a pretty obvious edge in my voice. "I'm hardly forcing your science into a metaphor."

"When light shines on dark matter it doesn't do anything; the light just passes through. So, in that sense it's dark, I guess. But it's not black because black things do interact with light—they absorb light."

"I didn't say—or even think—it was black. That would be literal and not metaphorical." There were times, such as this, when Miriam acted as though she were smarter than me and it was annoying. "I meant dark matter is unknown and therefore unsettling," I said, "at the very least."

"Right. All I'm saying is dark matter isn't some diabolical thing. It's just that we can't detect it yet."

"So, it is unknown," I said triumphantly.

"True," she said. "It interacts with gravity, so in huge amounts it's powerful." She shrugged. "My periods of feeling low aren't the reason I was drawn to dark matter. It's actually not connected in my mind to feeling dark at all, metaphorically speaking. You know, in the history of the universe, huge, huge amounts of dark matter collapsed and collected to create galaxies, and these led to the formation of stars. And stars, of course, as they form and collapse, create life as we know it."

"The darkness brought us light?" I asked.

"No," she said, laughing. "But you could say—with some qualifications—that the darkness brought life."

As I was saying, the summer before Miriam met Andrew, she had been in the Lows. It was prior to her second year at university and she was feeling uninspired. Enrolled in a math program she wasn't enjoying, she had decided to switch to part-time and was considering quitting university altogether. But immediately before fall term, when the weather turned, she felt good again and signed up for an astronomy course, which, it turns out, is what Andrew was teaching.

Andrew was the one who suggested she pursue astrophysics. Looking back, this might have seemed an obvious choice, considering that when we were growing up seemingly everyone wanted to travel to outer space. Those were the years soon after the Apollo missions and the moon landing, when most elementary classrooms had a model of a rocket that came apart so the teacher could demonstrate how it worked, from takeoff to re-entry. Movies and television shows like *Star Wars* and *Battlestar Galactica* were popular. Most every boy I knew in those days wanted to be an astronaut for a time, including Saif and Salim. Salim, in particular, was obsessed with outer space, so much so that when Miriam first told me she was going in this direction, I wondered if it was about him. But that wasn't it. She really was interested, not in a childish fantasy of becoming a Jedi Knight, but in the questions underlying the universe. Andrew showed her some real options and a concrete career path.

"Did you know the moon is in free fall?" she asked me one night, not long after she and Andrew had become a couple.

"What do you mean? It's falling out of the sky? Are we all about to die?"

"No. It's in constant free fall as it goes around the earth."

"So then," I said, "this is another way of saying it's in orbit?"

"Kind of," she said. "The balance of the moon's speed and earth's gravity creates what we call orbit. If the moon were moving faster than it is, it would fly away; if it were slower, it would hit the earth. But isn't it funny that what we think of as a passive sensation, falling, is actually a pull? We don't feel gravity when we're falling because we only feel a force when we resist it. But it's an *attraction*," she said, emphasizing the final word. "In other words, we don't fall in love. Love pulls us toward itself."

"It's still passive from our perspective. We are being pulled by love."

"You're right!" she said with what I felt was an unwarranted degree of enthusiasm. "Love is running the show."

At this point, I understood why Miriam was going on about attraction and falling and the power of love. She was determined to prove what we both knew wasn't true—that she was in love with Andrew. When she spoke of him, she didn't become excited about him. She became excited about the courses he suggested and the grad schools he recommended, and she became really excited about the science he discussed with her: supernovas and black holes and that type of thing. She hardly talked about Andrew the person at all. I think she needed to believe she was in love to justify her decision to move in with him, which she had decided to do a few days before this particular conversation. You see, Miriam actively disliked her roommate in residence and had been desperate to find a living arrangement she could afford off campus. Andrew lived in a house with a group of graduate students. Moving in with him was a convenient arrangement. In other words, Andrew wasn't the pulling force; her annoying roommate was the push. Love had nothing to do with any of it.

It's funny. I reminded Miriam about this conversation when we were on Vancouver Island years later. I was visiting her and Zara, who was a toddler then, at the house where Miriam was living with Zara's father, Peter. It was nighttime and she and I were looking through a telescope in the living room when I brought it up.

"You're misremembering," she said. "I wouldn't have said that."

She was grumpy, convinced at that time Peter was cheating on her and so she was particularly sour on love. I wasn't surprised she refused to acknowledge it.

"You did say it was a force that pulls," I said, "like magnets."

"Gravity and magnetism are completely different forces," Miriam said. "I did not say that."

"Okay, maybe not the magnet part," I said.

"Whatever I said, I take it back. Okay?" she said. "I was full of shit."

I want to tell you more about that visit, but I'll get to it later. First, let me get back to telling you what happened between Miriam and Andrew. By the time she was in summer term, Miriam had broken up with him and was dating another graduate student, a guy who lived in the house with them. During a two-week stretch when Andrew was out east visiting his parents, she had packed up her things from his bedroom and moved them into the other guy's room down the hall.

When he returned home, Andrew exploded. The two guys had a big fight, throwing punches and everything. Clearly Miriam and her new guy—I don't even remember his name, Matthew or Mark or something (I do recall it was a New Testament name)—had to move out of the house immediately. At the time, I was surprised she hadn't anticipated the drama that would ensue from her decision to simply switch boyfriends. But now that I think of it, of course Miriam knew it would go badly. She simply didn't care. It wasn't about the guys; they were a means to something, namely housing and career advancement. By the fall semester Miriam was back in a dorm because she and Matthew/Mark were kaput.

But a weird development during all of this was that after Miriam split up with him, Andrew started to call me. The first time he phoned he was so drunk he was having trouble forming words, but he was coherent enough to beg me to ask Miriam to give him another chance. I knew there was no point in this, but I promised him I'd talk to her, which I did. I suggested she meet him for coffee or something, just to make sure he was okay. She laughed and said I should ignore him if he called again. I tried to do this, but he was insistent.

The truth is, I didn't mind talking to Andrew. He called me a few times a week for a month or so, repeating that Miriam had crushed him, that she had used him (according to him—and Miriam confirmed this—she had not paid any rent during the four months that she stayed in his room) and discarded him like he was nothing. After our talks I would sit up for hours, late into the night, feeling horrible on his behalf. At one point Miriam asked me if I was in love with him. I told her I was worried he was having a breakdown, which I was. Until these talks with Andrew, I had never had a meaningful conversation with a man. In retrospect I think I enjoyed the attention he was giving me, even though it wasn't at all about me. But during our calls I had come to think of myself as a bit of a wise counsellor. I believed I was helping him and that he needed me. To suggest I was in love with him was overstating it, of course, but there was a moment here or there when I imagined he would end up falling for me, like in a movie. But I didn't let myself fantasize too far because it would be a betrayal of Miriam.

Then one day Andrew told me he had met someone new, and he sounded happy. But as he was talking he suddenly went over a cliff. He started crying and said as wonderful as this new woman was (he had earlier listed all the ways she was superior to Miriam: a lecturer with a completed PhD, kind, considerate, beautiful), she wasn't Miriam. No one could be.

"What is so great about Miriam?" I blurted. "Really, you need to enlighten me because I'm not seeing it. Either she has some qualities she's kept hidden from me or you are completely nuts."

Miriam laughed when I told her what I'd said. But Andrew, who hung up after I said that, never called me again.

"What a relief," Miriam said. "He's such a loser."

You can imagine my surprise when, a year and a half later, Miriam told me Andrew had written a reference letter for her master's applications. "We're still in touch. He's very supportive of my career," she said in response to my stunned silence.

I met Andrew in Toronto a few years after that, when he attended a conference where Miriam was delivering a paper. By then she was engaged to be married, and she introduced her fiancé to Andrew while I stood next to the three of them. I smiled, but Andrew stared at me blankly, pretending not to have a clue who I was. Miriam was in a giddy state of mind, having just finished her presentation; she didn't remind him who I was and instead perfunctorily introduced us as though we'd never met. I remember feeling humiliated and a bit confused. I can still see the scene. The four of us standing in a hall in University College, the wooden floorboards gleaming and light streaming through those gorgeous huge windows while they laughed and talked, the men hovering around Miriam like they were lowly planets and she was the glorious sun. I'm not sure what I was in this metaphor; I suppose I was empty space.

Chapter 12

WHEN I TOLD you, just now, that sometimes I felt Miriam acted as though she were smarter than me, it sparked a memory about a conversation she and I had over the phone about six years ago. She was living with Peter and no longer teaching or researching. Her life revolved around Peter and his sons and particularly around Zara, who would have been a few months old then. At one point during the call, Miriam asked me if I knew about Schrödinger's Cat, which was an absurd question. Of course, I knew. This is probably the most famous thought experiment in existence, and Miriam and I talked about it a lot—and in depth—over the years, including her mentioning it during the speech she gave for Ben and me. Once when I was visiting her at UBC, Miriam wanted to go to a Halloween party on campus and she insisted we dress up as Schrödinger's Cat. It was a fairly easy—not to mention comfortable—costume so I was on board. Each of us dressed in a black turtleneck and blue jeans and wore black hairbands onto which we attached little pointy ears cut out of paper. I used black eye pencil to colour the tip of my nose and draw whiskers onto my cheeks. While I was doing this, Miriam took some liquid eyeliner and painted an impressively straight line over each of her eyelids, flicking it out and upwards at the outer edges. I had seen photographs of my mother in the 1960s wearing this style of makeup. She looked like the Hindi film star Meena Kumari. I loved the look and was disappointed it wasn't in fashion when I became an adult. I was amazed to see Miriam doing her eyes this way and asked her to do the same for me. She happily obliged.

"You look gorgeous," she said when she was done. To my surprise, as I stared at my face in the mirror, I didn't completely disagree.

Finally, we each taped a piece of paper on the front of our turtlenecks. Mine read "Alive" and hers read "Dead." Or maybe it was the other way around. I can't recall.

"We are Schrödinger's Cat," I explained that evening to a nice-looking young man who had been staring at us ever since we walked into the party.

"What?" he said, moving closer to me.

"A physicist named Schrödinger came up with this experiment, which he actually never carried out,"

I said. "That's why it's called a thought experiment."
I bit my lip, realizing he probably knew what a thought
experiment was. Mercifully he nodded slowly, which
I interpreted as a signal to continue. "A cat is in a box
with a vial of poison and an atom in a state of decay.
When the atom decays it will release a radioactive electron, which will then cause a contraption of sorts to
knock over the vial of poison gas and kill the cat. But it
is equally possible the atom will not decay and release
the electron and the cat will live."

I couldn't tell by his expression whether he was
confused or not, but he was staring with furrowed
brow, so I kept talking.

"Here's the thing," I said, "you can't see inside the
box. You won't know whether cat is alive or dead—"

"—until you open it?" he said. I nodded, smiling.

"No," Miriam said. "It's in a state of quantum superposition until it is observed. It's actually neither dead
nor alive. Or both dead and alive." She wiggled her
index finger between my sign to hers. "Like us."

I probably should have been more embarrassed that
I didn't really understand the difference between what
I had said and what Miriam had said. Instead, I was
feeling quite pleased that I had correctly remembered
as much as I had and, more importantly, that I had
held this guy's attention. But then I noticed that he was
looking intently at Miriam, and she was looking back
at him. I want to say she was purring but I know this
is ridiculous. But she was staring at him in a way that

seemed to have locked him into her. I walked away and found a bathroom. I didn't need to use it, but I didn't know what else to do, so I stared at myself in the mirror. My eyeliner had smudged and become a black blotch over each eye. (Had I rubbed my eyes at some point?) I didn't look attractive at all. I looked frightening, like a ghoul. I wet some toilet paper to wipe it off but this only made it worse. I gave up and wandered out, catching up with Miriam a few minutes later. She showed me a slip of paper with a phone number.

"Will you call him?" I asked.

She shook her head. "You want it?"

I stared at her in disbelief. "Why would I want it? He gave you his number, not me. He's obviously not interested in me."

"How could he give it to you? You disappeared," she said. "And isn't the point that you're interested in him?"

"I'm not calling a guy who was gawking at you. I have some pride."

Then she said something like, "You need to focus on what you want."

I don't remember her words exactly because I was pretty annoyed with her. First she flirted with a guy I was interested in, and then she expected me to be grateful that she got his phone number.

I seem to have gone off track. The only thing I had intended to convey with this story is that Miriam must have been aware that I knew Schrödinger's Cat experiment very well. And yet that day over the phone, while she was living with Peter and baby Zara, she asked me whether I knew it. Her question ought to have alerted me that something was off with her. But over the previous year and a half or so Miriam had been behaving less and less like herself, so very little she did or said surprised me. It annoyed me, certainly. But it didn't concern me.

The aim of her existence during those days was to create a family with Peter, Zara, and Peter's two sons. It wasn't working out. For one thing, Peter's father, who had recently had a fall and who openly hated Miriam, was living in the house with them. The second and bigger issue was that Miriam was no longer working at all. When she was pregnant with Zara, she took an unpaid leave of absence from her postdoc at the University of British Columbia. The time to return was well past. She simply set aside her research, her life's work, in order to play the role of matriarch in this broken family. If I tried to broach any of this, she refused to discuss it, assuring me—in a nonchalant voice—that it was under control. So, to be honest, I gave up worrying about her life. I would listen when she called, and I would provide updates about my life if she expressed any interest in knowing.

"A scientist named Wigner took this experiment further," Miriam said after I assured her I knew all about Schrödinger's Cat. "This thought experiment is called Wigner's Friend and it goes like this: I'm Wigner's friend and I'm in a lab observing the cat in the box. I have opened the box, but you—you are Wigner—are outside my lab. You know I've looked inside the box but you don't know the result that I know."

"So, this is Schrödinger's Cat Part Two?" I said. "Why not call it Wigner's Cat then? Instead of Wigner's Friend?"

"A couple of reasons," she said. "One is that the friend is central to this experiment. And second, Wigner actually used an example of a photon. I'm using the cat because it'll be easier for you to understand."

"I can understand the photon example, Miriam."

"Can you?"

Again, she seemed to forget everything we'd ever discussed. For decades Miriam and I used to have these conversations about physics wherein she would teach me something using an informal, Socratic question-and-answer method. Sometimes I wasn't in the mood but mostly I enjoyed it; quantum physics is a trip and Miriam's enthusiasm about her work was infectious. I mean, it had been a long time since we'd discussed physics specifically, certainly not since she'd met Peter, but there was no need for her to behave as though she hadn't spent the past decade educating me on quantum theory and objective reality and anything else that she had obsessed about.

"We change reality when we observe it," I said. "Particles exist in a state of probability, like waves, until we observe them. A photon's interaction with us—it must hit our eye for us to observe—alters what we are seeing."

Okay, I probably didn't state it this perfectly back then, but I know I had the gist of it because I did understand wave particle duality. There was no reason for Miriam to act as though she had to dumb it down for me.

"All right, okay, good," she said. "I'm sorry. Back to Wigner's Friend. From your perspective outside my lab, the whole of my reality is in superposition, still within many possible states. It has not yet collapsed into reality. So, whose point of view is more valid? Wigner's or Wigner's friend's? Yours or mine? For me, in the lab, the wave has collapsed into a particle. It is now fixed reality. For you it is still probabilistic."

"I can see you. You can't see me," I said. "I am godlike."

"Not godlike," she said. "I know something you don't know. I have measured. You have not. You cannot."

"Okay, then, equally valid. Our points of view are equally valid. Neither of us has all the information."

"Right," she said. "But this introduces a paradox. My wave function has collapsed. My reality exists. But yours does not, not yet. When is reality formed?"

"Your reality is formed when you observe it and my reality is formed when I observe it," I said in response to her question. "Is that what Wigner was trying to say with this experiment?"

"What he's conveying is there is no objective reality without consciousness," she said. "Your consciousness. Only yours exists."

"Only my reality exists *for me*," I clarified.

"What else is there?"

"Beyond my perspective, you mean?"

"Perspective implies there are multiple ways to observe one thing, one objective reality," Miriam said. "But like you said just now, without observation there is no reality. Literally."

"Okay, I get it," I said. "Even though you, my friend, have observed in your lab and thus your reality has formed, for me my reality won't form until I have observed you."

"Correct. I am in a state of superposition, both dead and alive."

"What does that feel like?" I said, laughing.

I didn't expect her to answer. It was a joke, a nonsensical question. But she said this: "Like hell. It feels like hell."

Chapter 13

MIRIAM CALLED ME in a strange state another time. It happened about a year earlier than the occasion I just described. She phoned me, drunk, at three in the morning. Well, for me it was three in the morning; for Miriam, on the West Coast, it was midnight. She apologized profusely when I reminded her about the time difference. I had been awake when she called—I used to suffer from some pretty serious insomnia back then—but I let her go on saying sorry for a bit. I know it was petty of me, but I had been annoyed with her selfish behaviour of late and I suppose I was trying to put her in her place. You see, at this point Miriam was in the early days of her affair with Peter. It wasn't her first affair, but it was the first time her lover had a wife and young children.

I couldn't understand how Miriam would mess up an entire family just to have yet another romance. But I didn't say anything then. Not long afterwards, I did let her know what I thought of her affair with Peter. But I'll get to that a bit later. First, I want to tell you what we discussed on this late-night phone call.

"I'm Peter's sauten," Miriam said.

"You're not pronouncing it correctly," I said. "It's not a hard English t. It's त. And you are not his sauten. You're his wife's."

"I thought sauten means mistress?"

"Not exactly," I said. "It does refer to a mistress, but it's one of those words you can't really translate. It defines the relationship between the women. A man's mistress is his wife's sauten. Maybe a better translation of sauten would be rival."

I should go back a bit and explain why I knew Hindi with more proficiency than Miriam. Hindi, like Gujarati and Punjabi, is an Indic language and so Miriam and I could more or less understand the gist of a basic Hindi conversation. She didn't know Punjabi as I did, though, because her parents were both Gujarati. So, I had a slightly wider linguistic base than she did. But additionally, and more importantly, while growing up I voraciously devoured Hindi films. I particularly loved Hindi film songs. In my determination to understand them, I wrote out the lyrics, cross-referenced words to discern their meaning, and thereby picked up more and more vocabulary. In the 1980s, when VCRS became popular, my parents would rent Hindi films on videotape and these (presumably because they were intended for audiences in North America) tended to come with English subtitles, which helped me learn even more. When I moved to Toronto for university, I took informal Hindi lessons with a classmate for about a year. She taught me not only how to speak the language but also how to read and write the script. I learned only to a rudimentary level, but that was good enough to make use of a Hindi-English dictionary. I really only wanted to be better at translating old film songs. I had pretty much stopped watching the actual films by then. In fact, I haven't seen one in years. Hindi films, at least when I last watched them in the 1970s and 1980s, tended to be melodramatic and pretty ridiculous at times, with over-the-top fight scenes and contrived plots. But the songs were always better than the actual films. The lyrics were sophisticated and the imagery rich. Some of the lyricists were bona fide Urdu poets.

But when I was a child, I wasn't admiring poetry or looking down on melodrama. Hindi films mesmerized me. Miriam said they were silly. She thought anything Indian was silly, to be honest. But she would still come to the movie theatre with my family whenever she was invited. She would sit in the back seat of my dad's big Oldsmobile with me and Saif for the drive to Gerrard Street in Toronto. Something about the trips must have drawn her. She'd probably say it was the popcorn and samosas. But during the film, particularly when the drama had reached a crescendo, I would steal a glance at Miriam and see that she was completely enthralled. It was hard not to be. Melodramas are emotionally captivating. And these Hindi films had romance and action and stunning scenery. But what really grabbed me was that they were an emotional roller coaster that ultimately ended in a satisfying way. The moral distinctions were clear. And good always prevailed. Sure, you'd see the hero suffer throughout the movie; sometimes he'd even die in the end. But right won; goodness won. Every time. The hero of the film was never a woman, by the way. I've thought about this a lot over the years as I've studied literature and come to understand narrative and character development. But as a child I didn't notice that the female characters were two-dimensional. I imagine there were probably some movies where the woman goes through some kind of arc and has a bit of nuance to her character, but I don't remember any. The women I recall were either good or bad. The good ones were chaste and passive and tended to keep their eyes lowered and their heads covered with the pallu of a sari. For being good, they would be rewarded with the title of wife. The bad one usually did a sexy dance or two, flirted with the hero, spoke her mind, and tried to use her beauty and sexual appeal to get what or whom she wanted.

The word Miriam brought up, sauten, came up a lot in the movies we watched. Many movies would have a sauten and a story arc about an affair. Ultimately, the good, chaste woman from a respectable family won the hero's love and respect. And the sauten, the bad woman with whom he shared a flirtation or had an affair, would simply disappear. The hero would reject her or ignore her and she wouldn't be around in the final scenes.

"So then what am I to Peter, in Hindi?" Miriam asked on the phone. "If not his sauten?"

"Rakhel, I guess," I said. "It literally means kept woman."

"Oh, wow. No. I'm not that. Isn't there another word? Like lover or something?"

"There are plenty of words for beloved," I said. "But if that's what you were after, why start with sauten?"

"Cat—his wife—confronted me today and called me a slut, which was a little bit funny, considering she's such an avowed feminist," Miriam said. "I wanted to tell her that I am not a slut; no woman is a slut. But it would be fair to say I'm his sauten." Then Miriam started laughing. "But apparently that would have been wrong."

I didn't laugh because I felt badly for Cat. Miriam had been Cat's friend before she started sleeping with her husband. Miriam may not have been a slut, but she was, as I say, selfish.

"You know," Miriam said, "I don't think rival is a good translation. It misses the mark. People are each other's rivals. We are not each other's sauten. I'm the sauten; she is the wife. If we were in an Indian movie," Miriam continued, "she would win the man, wouldn't she?"

"But we're not in an Indian movie," I said.

Miriam laughed again and I think she said that's a good thing or something like that. The call ended there, or any meaningful discussion did, in any case. I came to realize pretty soon after this conversation that while rival wasn't an accurate translation of sauten, Miriam did see Cat as her rival.

One of the last times I saw Miriam, after Cat had died and Miriam and her daughter had moved into the house Cat had shared with Peter, the one overlooking the ocean with the huge windows and the high ceilings, she rambled on and on about Cat in a kind of stream-of-consciousness rant. It was late October and for some reason I cannot recall, we were outside near the water. As she talked, the waves pounded against the rocks, as though to punctuate the emotion behind her words.

"Cat had all that pedigree. English and a WASP. Private schools. Our dads, I mean, come on, with their Indian accents and no education. Can you imagine what it was like for her? What is it like to be white and rich and your father is some big shot and you go to the most expensive private school? I saw him a few times, the old man, the way he looked at me. I don't know. All that hate. I mean, I guess who could blame him? But with everything she had, Catherine the Great, she still moaned and was depressive. What the fuck was her problem? How do you feel worthless when you're told you're everything? She was on antidepressants and in therapy with a life like that. If I had a mom or dad and teachers and advertisements and every goddamned thing telling me how special I am—what does that feel like?

"And then Peter married her, in that fancy wedding, and she was his queen and his family welcomed her and adored her and made her theirs. And they won't talk to me. When Peter's dad lived here, he wouldn't talk to me or even look at me. Can you imagine? That's why Zara and I left. Peter suggested it. Just for a while, he said. It was too much for his father. Okay, I get it, his father thinks I'm trash, but what about Zara? She's your blood, a total innocent. But nope. I mean why would her grandfather treat her like a human being when Peter won't even treat her like his daughter?

"I do this thing. I imagine life in Cat's skin. Her white skin and her auburn hair and light blue eyes. Rich girl, going to private school. So damn fucking gloriously lucky! I'm not suggesting Peter's dad or anyone is treating me like trash because I'm not a white princess with pedigree. I know it's because I'm the other woman. I'm just saying, what was it like to be Catherine, to be the right person in the right place, every day of your life?"

"Is that why you live in her house, sleep in her bed, mother her sons, play wife to her husband?" I said this. I said these words. I didn't only think them. But the waves must have swallowed them because Miriam didn't respond.

The next day, when I was on a ferry headed to the Lower Mainland, I remembered a girl from elementary school. Her name was Jane. She wasn't pretty. But I didn't realize this until much, much later. I think I was in my mid-twenties when I realized Jane was unattractive. She was scrawny and covered in freckles and had stringy hair. Her eyes were beady and her lips were thin. She was just an unfortunate-looking wisp of a thing. But she was a year older, or a grade ahead in any case, and in elementary school that is power. But it wasn't the age that blinded me to her looks. It was that she was white. Being white meant you didn't have to be all that pretty; you were automatically prettier than me, for example, just having the right colouring. Anyways, one day I was leaving school late. I had helped the teacher clean the blackboard and it was four p.m., when in winter the daylight already wanes. I remember this because I looked at the clock and saw that I had been there for fifteen minutes after the final bell. I walked out the school doors to an empty schoolyard, wearing my powder-blue snow pants. They were small for me. The ankles of my black boots were exposed but I didn't mind because that day was bitterly cold and the pants were keeping me warm. And then Jane materialized.

"Hey Paki, you shit your pants."

I knew that she was referring to the mud on the seat of my snow pants. They were old and I went tobogganing a lot, even on days when there wasn't a lot of snow. So, they were stained.

But I wasn't about to explain this to her. I kept walking and pretty soon she was directly behind me. I could hear her breathing.

"Paki, I'm talking to you."

I walked, my head lowered. I wasn't scared. She was quite a bit smaller than me. But I was embarrassed. I hoped that if I ignored her, she'd just leave me alone.

But instead she kicked me in the bum. I continued walking. She kicked me, again and again, harder each time. She kicked with such force at one point that my lower back arched. I didn't fall, because, as I say, she wasn't very big compared to me. I kept walking, my head lowered and my eyes hot with tears. Eventually she stopped kicking me and, I suppose (because I didn't look to see where she went), turned around and left.

"Why didn't you kick her back? Or go find a teacher? Who is she? Let's go find her." This is what Miriam said when, a year later, I told her what happened. But Jane wasn't even at my school anymore. She went to middle school now. And I had no clue where she lived.

Something else happened with Jane, though I didn't share this incident with Miriam or anyone. This was before the kicking incident, in the fall, but the memory came to me afterwards. A few of us—somehow Jane was part of it—had decided to create a cheerleading squad. We didn't have cheerleaders in our school. I think we got to talking about setting up a squad because of an episode of *Happy Days* that had aired the week before. I was pretty excited. We decided to make up cheers, and I knew I was good at that kind of thing, so I already started thinking of lines. And some of the girls were planning what we could wear, and I thought my long legs would look good in the short skirts I saw cheerleaders wear on television. A day or so later, a few minutes before our first practice, one of the girls, I can't recall who, told me Jane said I couldn't be on the squad. According to this girl, Jane said it was because I was a Paki.

I don't remember what I said or if I said anything. A few minutes later, I watched from a distance as they practised on the soccer field. A couple of weeks after this, during the boys' first soccer game of the season, the cheerleaders, including Jane, clad in winter coats and long pants because the temperature had dropped precipitously, bounced up and down awkwardly on the sidelines, screeching incoherently. The only people looking at them were laughing. It was satisfying to see them look like idiots after they had kicked me off the squad. But I didn't feel good. The only feeling I remember from that day was a tight sensation in my gut, like an invisible hand was gripping my insides. Looking back, I realize what I was feeling was the discomfort of recognizing I agreed with Jane: a Paki can't be a cheerleader.

I'm telling you about Jane to explain that I understood what Miriam was saying about Cat. I did. I absolutely sympathized. A small part of me even relished the fact that Miriam could steal Cat's privileged life. But I knew—and Miriam knew too—she would never be the wife. No matter how well she took care of Peter's sons, no matter how many meals she cooked for Peter's father, no matter even that she was the mother of Peter's child. She would always be the sauten.

Part II

Collapse

Chapter 14

MIRIAM WAS MARRIED twice in her life. Her first marriage, to a graduate student in Toronto, ended after less than a year, amicably, but more Miriam's choice than his. They had married impulsively when they were quite young, so the divorce wasn't too surprising. But because it was Miriam, she made the whole process messier than it needed to be; by this I mean she started seeing a new guy before she had split up from her husband. But on the whole, everyone came out of it more or less unscathed.

The second time she married, Miriam was older, and I do think in this case they had a solid relationship, one that could have lasted a long time if Miriam would have put in the effort. It was an unlikely union, for sure. First of all, Jai was a musician. Miriam had only ever been in serious relationships with academics or scientists. The second thing was that he was South Asian. Despite being South Asian herself, Miriam had never dated one before, not even casually.

Jai, who had immigrated to Canada from India when he was in his late teens, played a North Indian classical instrument called a sarangi. It's a string instrument that makes a beautifully haunting, mournful sound. I love it—it plays in the background of many Hindi film songs—and would sit mesmerized when I listened to him practising. Jai told me that he fell in love with the sarangi because it is almost always an accompanying instrument. He never wanted to be a soloist.

"I wasn't born for that," he told me. "I was born to be in the background." I remember clearly when he said those words because that's when I understood why he and Miriam were attracted to each other.

Although he shied away from the spotlight, Jai was an accomplished musician. In India there is something known as the guru-shishya parampara. It translates more or less to the "master-disciple tradition" and Jai spent four years in it. He began to live and train full time with his guru when he was only ten years old. The guru-shishya tradition is an entire lifestyle. Jai explained that every facet of his life was geared towards learning and perfecting the art form. Sometimes he would do mundane and degrading jobs, such as washing the floors or his guru's clothes, but he would have to trust this was all in service to his art. When he was taught actual music he would spend months and months on one simple movement.

"I had to surrender my ego for art," Jai told me once, shaking his head. "But my ego refused."

Practically, this meant that after a number of contentious and unpleasant years, Jai left his guru. He never became a master, but he was a wonderful artist. Jai earned money fixing computers at a small shop in downtown Vancouver, but his real love was his band. It was called Dharm and it consisted of Jai on sarangi, another guy on tabla, a classical guitarist, and a female vocalist. They had cut one CD and managed to book quite a few shows at small venues and music festivals.

As I told you earlier, Miriam was not at all interested in anything Indian. And, so, were it not for me, she would never have met Jai, which she did one summer when I was living in Toronto and she was in town for a cousin's wedding.

At the time I was dating a guy named Josh. We'd only been on a few dates over a period of about three months, so it wasn't accurate then (or now) to call it a relationship. A colleague of mine (whose husband knew Josh from high school) had set us up on a blind date and, to be honest, I didn't think that first meeting went all that well. We had a few awkward silences, and I didn't find him particularly attractive. But the next day, he sent me some really beautiful flowers and then called and suggested we go out again. So, I agreed. After that we'd go out somewhere—dinner, to see a movie or a play—once a week or so.

Josh's wife had left him for a woman, which he told me within the first ten minutes of meeting, and he had only recently finalized his divorce. His ex-wife was all he really wanted to talk about. Okay, I'm exaggerating. Obviously, we talked about other things. He was a high school English teacher and he liked to see plays in little theatres throughout the city or to watch foreign films at repertoire cinemas. But no matter what the conversation was about, we always seemed to end up talking about his ex-wife. How she directed the staging of a Stoppard play at university, how she always overcooked pasta but made the perfect steak, how she changed the locks on their apartment after the separation without telling him, how they used to go to her family's place in Muskoka and skinny dip. Whenever we were having sex, I'm pretty sure he was pretending I was her. He didn't say anything, but he had this sad, faraway look in his eyes the whole time and if I tried to make eye contact he avoided it. But he did things like hold the door open for me or buy me chocolates and send me flowers for no reason at all, so I figured he was a pretty good catch.

While Miriam was in Toronto, the three of us went to an Italian restaurant on Queen Street and shared a wood-fired pizza. Josh was nice to her, asking about her work and about growing up in Kitchener. He even insisted on paying for the dinner. Overall, I thought it had gone well. After Josh went home, I was feeling pretty good because it was usually Miriam with a guy and me the third wheel. But as soon as she and I were in my apartment alone, before we had even taken off our shoes, she grabbed my shoulders and turned me to face her, really dramatic, like we were on a soap opera.

"Are you even physically attracted to this guy?" she asked. "At all?"

I stared at her.

"He's so fake and you guys are awkward together. Why are you with him? He's not good enough for you, not in looks or intelligence. God, some of the things he says. What was he going on about with that Baroque music crap? Were we supposed to be impressed? The guy is obviously intellectually insecure. You look bored when he talks. Which, who wouldn't be? He is boring."

I was quiet for a few moments. I couldn't think of how to respond. To be honest, I couldn't think at all because I was so stunned. At some point I finally said something like, "I can't believe you're saying this to me." But this didn't stop her.

"Are you?" she asked.

"Am I what? Bored? Yeah, sometimes. But you bore me too. Sometimes."

"No. Are you physically—sexually—attracted to him?"

"Yes, we have sex, Miriam. Jesus."

"I know you do. But do you really want him? Like, are you hot for him? Or are you going through the motions because you think that's what people do in relationships?"

I kicked off my shoes and went into the living room. "So, you're the only person who knows how to be in a relationship?" I said, turning to face her. "I have to fake being a normal person. Is that it?"

"I'm sorry," she said. "I didn't mean it like that. I mean you deserve better. You should really, really want to be with a guy. I don't know why you can't see that. You deserve a guy who makes you feel excited. I don't mean only sex. All of it. When he talks, it should be fascinating or funny or something. Not boring. And he should listen to you, not just drone on like the dull, self-absorbed high school teacher he is."

"Everything isn't passion," I said. "People in relation-ships can be normal and talk and sometimes be bored."

"Not in the first weeks," she said. "This is the wild-ride part."

"My parents learned to love each other," I said.

"Oh my God," she said and stared at me with her mouth gaping.

I rolled my eyes and walked away, sitting down on the sofa. She continued standing there as I picked up a *New Yorker* and pretended to read it.

"That was an arranged marriage," Miriam said, standing over me. "You want your parents' marriage? Seriously?"

"I'm just saying there are different ways to get to a good place."

"What place?" she asked. "If you're miserable now, won't you be miserable when you get wherever it is you think you're going?"

"I don't want to talk about it anymore, if that's okay with you," I said. I was angry but at the same time I felt really tired, so when I spoke my voice sounded kind of pathetic, as though I might cry, even though, honestly, I didn't feel like crying.

"Okay, yeah, sure," she said.

I'm suddenly reminded of a strange conversation I had with my father when I was twenty-one. We were driving somewhere; I can't recall where and it isn't important to this telling. I was in the passenger seat and he was driving, and he said, with no warning that this was coming, "You are now of marrying age."

I laughed. It was a ridiculous statement in so many ways that I thought it must be a joke. My father had never even hinted to me that I ought to be married off. Sure, my parents had a more or less arranged marriage. But this was never the expectation for me or Saif. Instead, my father encouraged us to go to university and establish careers of some sort. He was a modern father, rather than an old-fashioned Indian one. For example, he would offer me a glass of wine here or there and let me take the car out whenever I wanted. He also paid for me to attend university and live alone in Toronto. I'm not aware of him suggesting immediate marriage to Saif when he turned twenty-one, and Saif had a long-term girlfriend. And, so, that day in the car, I laughed.

My father became angry. "This isn't funny," he said.

He stared silently at the road with a furrowed brow—a scowl even—and I felt a bit sick to my stomach. I don't recall talking at all about anything for the rest of the ride. Obviously, I didn't marry at twenty-one. I've never been married. Less than a year after that conversation, my father died. He succumbed to a relapse of the cancer that first came when I was a child, the cancer that had foiled my mother's plans to leave him.

Miriam came to spend some time with me in the days after my father died and suggested we go to a party in Toronto a week or so after the funeral. I felt guilty because we were still in the forty-day mourning period. But my mother insisted I go for a few days and try to relax. At this party, I ran into a boy I had known in first year, the same one I slept with in an effort to get my virginity out of the way. I had managed to avoid him pretty much completely for the past few years. But he appeared at this party—walking towards me no less—like an apparition. I became a bit irrational, even panicked.

I whispered to Miriam, "He's the guy I lost my virginity to—what do I do?" He was standing almost directly in front of us at this point, his eyes on me.

"Say hi," she said in a firm whisper as she stared straight ahead. I obeyed. He smiled and we chatted a bit, nothing major. Just normal people talking about grad school and how he would never in his life consider it. That type of thing. Then he walked away and continued mingling. No big deal. But I remember it so clearly. It felt like a victory, and Miriam was the one who led me to it.

Later that night, she literally had to lead me around because I became really drunk. The scenes near the end of that night have become disjointed fragments in my mind. Miriam pulled me by the elbow and led me to the street. She hailed a taxi by whistling loudly, with her thumb and forefinger in her mouth. At one point during the ride, the driver had to stop. I must have said I felt sick, so he pulled over and I threw up on the curb. Surprisingly he let us back into the taxi because I remember singing along to a Leonard Cohen song that was playing on the radio.

I'm pretty sure Miriam joined me for the lines about laughing and crying, but I could be wrong. I also think I'm wrong about when I threw up. It was after I sang. Because now that I think of it, the taxi driver didn't let us back in after I retched on the curb.

Once again, I've strayed further than I had intended. I was telling you about the time Miriam met Jai. After she stopped grilling me about him that night, we ate ice cream and watched television. We didn't discuss my love life any more.

As it turns out, a month later, Josh called me and over the telephone said it would be best if we broke up. He admitted he was not over his wife and was going to start therapy. I was surprised that I didn't feel badly at all. I felt relieved. I didn't tell Miriam, then or ever, that he had dumped me; I said it was a mutual decision, which didn't feel entirely untrue. Anyways, that night, after she said all that to me about Josh, she felt a bit guilty I think and so she agreed to go to an Indian music festival with me the next day. That's where Jai was on stage with his band, Dharm.

The band was really good, and Jai, even though he was sitting off to one corner of the stage, was the best part of it. I loved the sound, as I say, of the sarangi and I was spellbound by the guy who was making it. He was young and good-looking and seemed oddly familiar I couldn't take my eyes off him the whole time. After the show Miriam and I were milling around outside the venue, where some tables had been set up for vendors. It was a hot summer night in the city and you could smell rotting fruit and vegetables. It's weird but lately, whenever I smell rotting fruit, I go back to that day, to standing outside on a warm summer night moments before I first saw Jai. I spent a lot of summers in downtown Toronto (when garbage day smells terrible), and of course I have smelled rotting fruit and vegetables on other occasions over the years. But these days whenever I do, I go back to that day.

Jai came out with his bandmates and started talking to people they seemed to know. He was taller than I had expected and his face was still flushed from the performance. I remarked to Miriam that he was cute. I was surprised when she agreed because she never said

Indian guys were attractive. I think at that point I said something to the effect of him being the type of guy who wouldn't be boring. I don't think she heard me, or maybe she was deliberately ignoring me, but she walked over to him and introduced herself. I followed but didn't initially speak up.

When he said his name was Jai, I realized why he looked familiar. "You look like Amitabh Bachchan," I blurted. "Exactly like when he played Jai, in *Sholay*!"

Miriam turned sharply to look at me. She was blushing and she widened her eyes, as though to indicate I should stop saying bizarre things.

"Tumhara naam kya hai, Basanti?" Jai said. And the two of us laughed.

"What does that mean?" Miriam asked.

"It means 'What's your name, Basanti?'" I said.

"That's what I thought," Miriam said, turning to Jai. "But her name isn't Basanti." Jai and I laughed again.

"What am I missing?" Miriam said. She was smiling, but I could tell she was annoyed.

Jai explained that it's a famous line from the Hindi film *Sholay*, uttered by a character named Jai.

Sholay was probably my favourite movie from childhood. It's a Western, believe it or not, with horses and gunfights in the desert. The story follows two small-time criminals as they take down an outlaw who is terrorizing a town, but at its heart it's about the unbreakable friendship between two men, one of whom is named Jai (I don't remember the other friend's name). I could have sworn Miriam had seen this movie as well; even Saif was a fan for a time. But it could be that my family saw it at the drive-in back in Nairobi when I was five or six. I can't recall. One of the main stars—the actor who plays Jai—was Amitabh Bachchan, my first childhood crush. He was charismatic and even though he had very few lines in *Sholay*, he stole all his scenes; the movie's success launched him into superstardom.

I was such a big Amitabh Bachchan fan that my parents took me to see him at Maple Leaf Gardens when I was twelve. He had come, along with the singer Lata Mangeshkar, for a big song-and-dance stage show. I clearly remember the outfit I wore that day: a white denim pantsuit with exposed brown stitching on the seams. I wanted Amitabh to like me, and he wore white jeans or pants a lot, or at least his characters did. Thinking about it now, I don't know why he was so attractive to me. The actor was my father's age and did not have the boyish looks that I usually liked. (For example, my other major childhood crush was Shaun Cassidy.) Amitabh wasn't a typical Hindi film romantic hero who had a genteel manner and conventional looks. Instead, he was extremely tall—almost awkwardly so, with large features and gangly limbs—and he tended to play angry young men who had spent their child-hood orphaned and living on the streets rather than among respectable people. He would often portray a criminal with a tender heart; he wanted to be good, but no one had ever taught him how. Eventually, this character would become respectable or die doing something heroic. Looking back, I think I was attracted to Amitabh because I identified with these characters: people who existed on the margins.

Obviously, Amitabh Bachchan didn't see me at Maple Leaf Gardens that day in 1981. It was a capacity crowd and our seats were far, far from the stage. From my perspective, he was a tiny figure way off in the distance, a figure who could have been anyone. But, still, I felt slightly stunned by the knowledge that he was there, in the flesh, rather than on a screen or in my head.

I was reminded of this feeling—or maybe a residue of it—when I saw Jai looking like a young Amitabh that summer evening. He was even wearing white jeans (and a kurta).

Jai and I shared our admiration for Amitabh and *Sholay* later, a year or so later, because on this day, outside the venue, Miriam homed in on him. After Jai and I had our short exchange about the film, she did that thing she would do where she would lock into a guy and ignore anything else around her, so I wandered over to a stall selling cheap silver jewellery. Miriam and Jai talked for such a long time that I ended up buying two rings I didn't want because I felt guilty I had wasted so much of the vendor's time. Later, Miriam told me she was absolutely smitten and that Jai lived in Vancouver so they were planning to meet up. I wasn't too surprised they had exchanged phone numbers. Miriam did this a lot. But I was surprised when they actually started dating.

Eight months later they had a small wedding, smaller than her first—which had been only about fifty people—but to my amazement she had a full Hindu ceremony, with a pandit and a fire and heaps of flowers and chanting for hours.

Miriam had abruptly stopped calling herself Mary when she started dating Jai. She was Miriam again, personally and professionally. This sudden about-face made me suspicious. It seemed to me she was playing a new role. Even at her wedding, I remember thinking she looked stunning but there was something not quite right about her appearance. She was wearing a red sari with gold embroidery that was draped over her head so that she looked demure, but she had a huge smile plastered on her face. Indian brides—at least in the films I've seen—tend not to smile. My mother didn't smile in any of her wedding photos either. So, maybe this is what made Miriam seem inauthentic to me. To be fair, Miriam was happy; that was real. She wanted to marry Jai. But she wasn't successfully pulling off the role of the shy Indian bride.

Chapter 15

THINGS WENT PRETTY well between Jai and Miriam for the first two years they were married. Miriam had another postdoc, so she was busy researching and Jai was doing his music and fixing electronics on the side. Sometimes he would come to Toronto for a show with his band. It was usually a short trip, no more than four or five days. Miriam would stay behind in Vancouver. I made it a point to watch him perform when he was in town, and we would usually chat for a bit afterwards. During these trips, Jai would sleep on a friend's couch to save money, but one time, at Miriam's request, he stayed at my house. I was living with Ben at the time, but he was away on a camping trip with his boys, so there was plenty of room for Jai.

Because I worked during the days and Jai was out of the house until late each night, I hardly saw him. But on the afternoon before his final show, he had a few hours to relax and I had a half day off, so I made him some chai. I was into making masala tea in those days and was always fiddling with recipes because I was determined to re-create the chai I'd had when I was in Delhi on a backpacking trip a few years earlier. On this occasion, I had used my mother's recipe with a few tweaks: I excluded the cloves and cut down on the amount of ginger. I remember this clearly because Jai said, with great flourish, that this decision made my chai superior to all the tea in Delhi.

"I hate laung, anyways," he said, using the Hindi word for clove.

"Did you know in Gujarati, laung is pronounced loving?" I said. As a child I had found this amusing.

Jai shook his head.

"I hate loving too," I said, and we both laughed.

As I'm telling you this now, it occurs to me it's not all that funny. Jai was probably only laughing to be polite. But this isn't the main thing I wanted to share about Jai's visit.

Miriam had told me that Jai came to Canada about twenty years earlier, when he was nineteen, to attend Humber College, and he then stayed on. It sounded like a pretty unremarkable story and, after she shared it, I didn't give it much thought. But on this day at my house—I can't remember how we came to be discussing the subject—Jai revealed that his travel to Canada, his student visa, his Humber College education, and even his application for permanent residency were all paid for by a white Canadian widow who was twelve years his senior. In return for all of this, she wanted him to be her lover. For years, she even covered the rent for a small bachelor apartment on Queen East, where she would visit him.

"Wow," I said. "Miriam didn't mention any of this to me."

"I have asked her to always let me tell this story," Jai said. "Or not tell it. I don't tell everyone. I'm not ashamed. But if people don't know me or how this situation came to be, it becomes salacious, a thing to gossip about."

Jai then went on to explain how the arrangement with his benefactress came to be. (I should mention that I was so unsettled by Jai's use of the word gossip that I never told Miriam he had shared this information with me.)

"She was in Delhi for a few days," he said, "heading to an Ayurvedic centre north of the city. I saw her—a flustered gori—arguing with a taxi driver. In fact, he was being very rude to her. I stepped in and—"

"You became her knight in shining armour," I said.

"Yes, that's right," he said, smiling. "After she returned from the Ayurvedic place, we spent a few days together. I took her on tours, the Red Fort, Gandhiji's resting place—tourist places, you know? But also to local restaurants. After that, about two months later, she returned and we took a trip to Darjeeling. It was a nice time. You know those days when you are falling in love and it feels like a dream? And nothing matters as it used to? She booked us at the Elgin Hotel."

"It sounds like a Merchant-Ivory film," I said, and this made him laugh.

"At this hotel," he said, "she first said I should move to Toronto." Jai shook his head. "I didn't take it seriously. I thought when she woke up from this dream, back at home, she would forget she had suggested it; she would forget even me. But after she returned home, she sent me application forms and described a plan, a good one, about where I could live, how she would help me financially, and how I could earn some money under the table." He shrugged. "And this is how I ended up here."

"Did you wake up from the dream?" I asked.

"Eventually, yes. But at the start, I was in love; I was very drawn to her."

"How did it end," I asked, "your arrangement with her?"

"Once I had my permanent residency status and I found a good job, I told her I was moving out of the apartment she was paying for. By then—this was now four, almost five years since we met—she was coming over less and less. It was time to end it. We parted as friends. I tried to pay her back over the years, but she always refused."

"Do you still talk to her?" I asked.

He shook his head. "I used to send her birthday cards

and flowers sometimes. One day—after I had sent her a card—she called and asked me not to do this anymore. She didn't say it in a bad way. She said we'd moved past needing or wanting each other. 'It's time to let it go and move on.' She was right. I was sending cards and gifts out of obligation."

"She sounds wise," I said.

"No," he said. "She isn't wise. I would say she is practical."

The conversation went on to some mundane things I can't recall and we sat on the sofa in the living room and sipped our chai. To clarify, I sat on the sofa; Jai sat in Ben's leather armchair. An old Hindi love song was playing in the background. (I had put on a CD earlier.) And we were quiet.

There were a couple of lines in the song that I couldn't quite translate, even with my Hindi-English dictionary, so, pausing the CD, I asked Jai about them.

"It's saying something about stars and falling. And darkness: I know that word," I said. "But I can't quite pull out the meaning."

"Basically," Jai explained, after asking me to replay the lines once more, "the singer is saying to his beloved that when she becomes distracted by the brilliance of the stars in the sky, she can longer see true light."

"Her own light?"

"No. The word means a greater light. The light of God. The light that dispels darkness. He assures his beloved that even when this happens to her, when she becomes lost in this darkness of her own making, she can come to him because this light will be there to guide her. It cannot be extinguished."

"Only obscured," I said.

He smiled.

We finished our chai and Jai went to the guest room to pack. A little later, as we stood in the front hallway, I stared at the top of his head as he zipped up his duffle bag.

"Did you date only white women?" I asked. "I mean, when you were living in Canada, after the widow?" I'm not sure why I asked him. The question left my mouth before I considered it. To this day, I'm not sure why I asked.

"Miriam isn't white," he said, not looking up.

"She passes for white," I said. "Lots of people think she's white."

He was quiet and was fiddling with his duffle bag for what seemed to me an unnaturally long time.

"I avoided dating Indian men, brown men," I said. "So, I was just wondering if you did that too. Like maybe this widow was attractive to you because she took you away from the world you knew and offered something—I don't know—different."

He looked up from his duffle bag and nodded. "Yes. I hadn't thought of it that way before, but I think you're right."

"There's a lot about the world I come from, the culture I come from," I said, "that I like."

"You can keep it," he said quickly. "Keep what you want, reject what you don't want. It's your life. There's no reason we should mindlessly repeat the lives our parents lived."

"My mother didn't date," I said. "I don't think she realistically expected me to date either. So, she didn't have an opinion on what I should do. White boys or brown boys. She didn't talk about it. She just talked about me one day being a wife, like it would just happen to me, the way I suppose it happened to her. I don't know what my father thought about the type of man I'd date or marry."

Jai was quiet.

"It would be nice not to be running away from things," I said. "And instead to be running towards things. You know?"

"Well," he said, standing up so that I was forced to look up at him, "sometimes you don't know where you're going. You know only that you need to go. That's okay too. It's okay to go. It's okay to leave."

I looked down at my feet. His words brought on a surge of emotion, and I didn't want him to notice.

"And now I must leave," he said.

This made me smile. And then we said goodbye. He was flying out late that night, directly after his show.

Chapter 16

THE ONLY REAL issue Jai and Miriam had in an otherwise harmonious marriage—at least for the first couple of years—was money, in that they didn't have a lot of it. But Miriam enjoyed the bohemian thing for a time, as I recall. She shopped at thrift stores and prided herself on how few things they needed. Despite this, her little apartment on the UBC campus became cramped. About a year and a half after they were married, they found a spacious two-bedroom flat off campus. It was the main floor of a house and was surprisingly affordable. The landlady was named Catherine, Cat for short, and she lived on Vancouver Island. She had inherited the house and recently converted it to a duplex. Cat immediately liked both Miriam and Jai. She not only rented them the flat, she also kept coming around and inviting Miriam for drinks or dinner and to see movies and art shows. Sometimes they would watch Jai's gigs.

Once, Miriam had to be in Victoria for some reason I can't recall and she spent the evening and overnight at Cat's. Cat and her husband, Peter, who was an architect, had a beautiful, sprawling house overlooking the ocean. That's the first time Miriam met Peter. She told me their initial encounter was electric. Instant heat. His dark eyes locked onto hers and didn't let go. (These were her words.) Their meeting was so charged, she told me, she felt a bit short of breath. We were talking over the phone so she couldn't see me rolling my eyes. She was well into her thirties now, so I thought this was all pretty juvenile. She went on about how gorgeous and masculine he was and how he kept stealing glances at her throughout dinner. He had already left in the morning with his children when she woke and then she had to leave herself, so she didn't see him again on that trip.

Miriam told me a number of times that Cat was one of those white women who was enamoured with holy Indian things. "Like the Beatles during their Hare Krishna stage," was how Miriam put it once. Cat was into yoga and talked about chakras and meditation, things in which Miriam had no interest.

She was always looking for meaning in a superficial way, Miriam explained, even with respect to Miriam's work. For example, once as they were sitting on the deck of Cat's house looking up at the night sky, she said, "Isn't it sad that stars have to die?"

"The death of a star isn't sad," Miriam told her. "It's spectacular."

She explained to Cat that dying stars bring about the elements—the ones in the periodic table, not some fanciful notions—critical to human life. But the biggest stars, the ones with the most mass of all, collapse into supernovas. "When a star dies in this way it has more energy than when it was a star," Miriam said. "No matter how it dies, the death of a star transforms the universe. It isn't sad. There's nothing sad about it," Miriam said.

She said Cat found this brilliant. "You are an absolute marvel, Miriam!"

Cat found Miriam marvellous and surprising, Miriam explained, because she held the view that Indian women were exotic and ethereal, not scientists who grew up in southern Ontario.

Cat wanted to know more and so Miriam took her to a lecture in the astronomy department at the university.

They had been friends for three or four months when Cat invited Miriam and Jai to Vancouver Island for a long weekend. Cat and Peter's two children were going to be with their grandparents, so it would be a grown-up gathering. On the Saturday afternoon, Miriam and Peter took a walk to the water while Jai and Cat stayed back at the house marinating paneer and chopping vegetables. Miriam told me, in far more detail than I will bother sharing here, how Peter kissed her as salt water sprayed over them. Later, Miriam learned that Cat had gone down to the water to call Peter for help starting the barbecue and saw the kiss. Cat didn't say anything to Miriam that day but clearly she was upset about something. She went to bed early, and later Miriam heard shouting from their bedroom, though she couldn't make out what was being said. In the morning Peter said Cat was still unwell, and Jai and Miriam took an early ferry back to the mainland.

Two days later Peter showed up at Miriam's office and told her that Cat knew about the kiss. She thought he was going to say it had been a mistake but instead he kissed her again, and they ended up agreeing that despite both their marriages, they needed to be together. But neither of them was ready to leave their partner, so they kept seeing each other secretly.

Regardless, because of the kiss, Miriam's friendship with Cat was over. Legally, Cat couldn't throw them out of the apartment, and Miriam wasn't ready to tip Jai off that anything was going on, so she didn't suggest they move from a home they loved. Each month, Miriam and Peter met up a few times in a Vancouver hotel, and she mailed a rent cheque to his house in Victoria, addressed to Cat.

One night, while Miriam and Peter were talking on the phone, Cat picked up an extension and listened in. She confronted her husband afterwards and they had a huge fight. The same night, Cat called Jai and told him about the affair.

He was devastated, Miriam told me. Despite this, he wanted to stay together, and Miriam agreed, for now. But he started sleeping on the sofa. A couple of months later, she discovered she was pregnant. She didn't lie to Jai. She told him she was about ten weeks along. They both knew the baby couldn't be his, based on the last time they had sex.

Chapter 17

A T THAT POINT in my life, I hadn't quite let go of the dream of an academic career and had applied for a position at the University of Victoria. They asked me to come for an interview, and I extended the trip for a few days so that I could visit with Miriam and Jai in Vancouver beforehand. When I got to her place, she told me Jai had moved in with a bandmate. Cat and Peter were living in the same house but only for the sake of the kids, Miriam explained. She hadn't decided if she was going to keep the baby, and so she and Peter decided not to tell Cat about the pregnancy.

"Jai is a good man," Miriam said as we sat in her living room. "But Peter is fire." She smirked when she said this, in that self-satisfied way she would do when she thought she'd won an argument. I remember thinking it was an apt metaphor; she was indeed playing with fire. But I suspected, as with other times, she would grow bored. She would terminate the pregnancy and her life would go on, with Jai or without. Though I didn't know what exactly she would do, of course, I got the feeling that she wasn't serious about Peter and it would end soon enough. But I felt absolutely terrible for Cat and her children.

"Peter tells me that whenever Cat talks about me, she calls me the Brown Dwarf," Miriam said. She was laughing, but I was quiet.

"People have awful names for their husbands' mistresses," I said, "which I kind of understand. But she could come up with one that isn't racist."

"No, no. It's clever," Miriam said. "A brown dwarf is a failed star. It's more than a planet, less than a star. They are the misfits of the universe."

"Misfits?"

"A failed star has more mass than a planet but not enough to ignite nuclear fusion in its core, which is what is required for a star to be a star. Not enough mass means not enough energy and so not enough light. Astronomers call this a brown dwarf. But do you see what I mean? They are in-betweens. It's clever."

"Cat knows this? I thought you said she was a financial manager or something." This is when Miriam told me how they had gone to that lecture about stars together.

I suppose it's possible Cat was using a term from astronomy about in-between stars. But Miriam told me that she was tall and had extremely pale skin. So maybe to her Miriam was a short brown thing. If I'm being honest, I wouldn't have blamed Cat if she were being especially cruel—even racist—with her nickname for Miriam.

"Cat dabbled in painting," Miriam said. "Did I tell you that? She has this beautiful studio in their house. And throughout the house, on walls everywhere, are all her dreadful pieces. She's talent-free. I'm actually embarrassed for her."

That's when I couldn't keep quiet any longer. "God, Miriam, you're pregnant with her husband's baby. She was your friend and you betrayed her horribly. How could you be so selfish? They have children. You're embarrassed for her? I'm embarrassed for you."

It was the first time in our entire friendship that I let Miriam have it like that. She was quiet and I braced for a counterattack, my heart pounding in my ears.

But she stayed calm. "She wasn't my friend," she said after a few moments, "not in any real way. Jai and I were like—I don't know—a curiosity to her. We were a pair of exotic zoo animals. We weren't real people. She only ever wanted to talk about something holy or deep or some such shit. Even with the astrophysics, it was always a surprise to her that I stuck to the science. At first she thought I was an astrologist and blathered on about the star she was born under."

This made me laugh and it eased the tension quite a bit.

"She wasn't my friend," Miriam said again. "I spent time with her because she invited me. She had a few tickets to good shows and she wanted to go to expensive restaurants she insisted on paying for. I don't know, I guess it was a break from my life of work and being poor. Maybe I used her in that way. But, no, not a friend. I wouldn't betray a friend like that. And Peter. I hadn't planned it. I don't know. Jai and I got married so fast. We are so different, and yeah, it was exciting at first, but it's been hard. I'm so tired of revelling in being poor. Plus, I'm sick of his musician friends."

"So, what will you do? Divorce Jai. Move in with Peter?"

"I don't know," she said. "Jai and I are done. That's obvious." Here she paused and looked at me for a few moments. "Sometimes, I have this thought that you and Jai were better suited for each other than he and I."

I felt my face become hot. "Then why did you aggressively flirt with him that first day we met him?" I said this angrily. And I was no less surprised than Miriam by my anger.

"What are you talking about?" she said. "You were interested in him?"

"You knew that," I said.

"How did I know that? I'm not Kreskin. My God, you don't realize how little you give away, do you? Do you expect people to be mind readers?"

"It doesn't matter," I said, quickly. "I was with Josh then, so it wasn't anything serious on my part. And you and Jai fell in love. I thought you were good together."

"We were," she said. "For a while. But Peter. I don't know. I want to be with him forever. I have never wanted a family, but I can imagine one with him. It's so weird. I can picture a family that includes those little boys of his."

I was shocked by this admission. Miriam had never expressed a desire for children. She had decidedly not wanted children. And now she was open to being a stepmother.

"Marriages end. They do," she said. "They end. I know I could have handled it better, but I love him. I love him."

This was a fairly kind version of events, this tragic love yarn Miriam was spinning. I know Miriam. I know that she kissed Peter that day to prove she was better than Cat. She can't have loved him yet. She didn't even know him. It was a game for her. But I allowed for the possibility that she had fallen for him. I'd never heard her say she wanted children or a family and this surprised me. I softened. I apologized for being harsh.

"That's okay," she said. "I get it. It looks bad." She was quiet and we sat on the sofa and said nothing for a while.

I was going to suggest we have some tea when Miriam brought up Cat again. "She sent me one of her pieces." She stood up and went into her bedroom, returning a few moments later with a small, framed painting. It was simple, a red handprint on canvas. "So, get this," she said. "Cat slipped and fell in her studio one day. It sounded like a scene from Laurel and Hardy the way she described it. Somehow her hand became coated in red paint and that same hand broke her fall by landing smack in the middle of a blank canvas. I saw the handprint in her studio, set by the wall ready for the trash—this was before the time Peter and I kissed, obviously—and Cat and I laughed about it, really laughed. And then I told her that it reminded me of a sati handprint. She had heard of sati, of course, but she didn't know about the handprints. When I told her, it moved her, which isn't surprising, because it's Indian and exotic."

I should explain to you what Miriam was talking about. Sati is the practice of widow immolation, something that used to happen in India, primarily in Rajasthan. And sati also refers to what a woman becomes when she immolates herself. Jauhar is related to sati and this is where the red handprint comes in. I learned about jauhar when I went backpacking through India about nine years earlier. During my master's degree I had taken a postcolonial literature course and became enthralled by South Asian novelists, in particular Salman Rushdie and Anita Desai. But I felt disconnected from India, particularly as my family was a couple of generations removed. And, so, I decided to travel there myself. My mother gave me the money to take a (low-cost) trip, so I picked up a Lonely Planet guide, bought a big backpack from Mountain Equipment Co-op, obtained a visa, and headed out with an open-ended return ticket.

Miriam told me more than once she thought this was a sad, crazy thing to do. "At least find someone to travel with," she said. "I'd come but it sounds really unpleasant."

I enjoyed travelling on my own. I didn't find it particularly lonely or sad. Sometimes I would meet up with people staying at the same hostel and we'd travel together for a few days. But most of the time, I was alone, including during my favourite portion of the trip, which was travelling through Rajasthan. It's a state next to my paternal ancestors' home state of Gujarat, but I don't think that's why I fell in love with it. I think its appeal for me was it seemed like something out of an ancient fairy tale. The state is mostly desert, but because it has been populated historically by a warrior caste, the Rajput, the landscape is dotted with sandstone forts. I spent a week in Jaisalmer Fort, which is an actual lived-in fort with turrets and bastions and huge fortified entrances. There are little shops tucked along the narrow walkways and, remarkably, an affordable hotel.

I took a few tours of forts throughout Rajasthan. On the walls at the entrance to many of these are small, red handprints. Sometimes the handprints are in neat rows but more often they are displayed in a haphazard fashion. I learned (first from tour guides and later from my own reading) that these handprints belonged to women who had participated in a ritual called jauhar. When Rajput warriors went to battle and were killed or likely to be killed, their wives would dress up in their bridal finery, dip their right hand in a vermillion paste, and then place the hand on the wall, leaving the red hand-print. After this, they would throw themselves into a mass pyre. The Rajput were, as I say, a warrior caste, and this act was seen as not only brave but also noble. It was a way for the women to avoid being captured and raped or enslaved by the enemy. Their bravery was seen as equal to the men's, who were ready to die in battle.

I became a bit obsessed with jauhar for a few months after I returned home. I read books about it and talked endlessly to Miriam on the subject. She was mostly dismissive.

"Sati is so horrible," I remember telling her once. "It signals to society that a woman has no value without a man. Jauhar tells a woman she does have value. Self-immolation ensures her value is not appropriated by the enemy."

"Your value is your virginity?" Miriam asked. "Or rather, your sexual purity is your value? I don't see a difference from sati. It's still women erasing themselves."

"But maybe there's something worse than death," I argued. "Maybe that's the point of it. For women in that situation in particular, they have no agency. But with jauhar they do. They can act. They can do something."

"But burn in a fire?" she said. "Death over dishonour. Honour before death. Better to be erased, to cease to exist, than to live with dishonour? That's horrifying."

"Not just dishonour," I said. "They would be enslaved. Death before enslavement. They are choosing their fate, aren't they?"

"No," she said. "There's no choice. What else could they do? Opt out and go live as single women? It's erasure," she said. "It's murder. No matter how you dress it up."

I told her she was right, but I wasn't convinced. Something about jauhar seemed different than sati to me. It's not that I admired it or anything; it horrified me. Maybe it's that I'd rather walk into a fire than be some man's slave.

After Miriam told Cat about jauhar, she briefly considered painting a scene of flames and a woman or multiple women burning in agony but decided it wouldn't honour women at all. It would simply glorify this terrible custom. In the meantime, Miriam had taken the canvas home and surprised Cat by having it framed.

"She loved it," Miriam said, "so much that she cried. And then after she found out about me and Peter, she had it sent to me, by courier." Miriam was holding the painting propped up on her lap, facing her. "I guess it was like giving me the finger."

Chapter 18

I SAW DHARM PERFORM at a bar the second evening I was at Miriam's in Vancouver. I went alone. "Jai has asked me not to come see them play," Miriam had said when I suggested we go together, "or to come see him at all. Also, I get tired in the evenings, nowadays. You go. I know how you love to watch him play his mournful music."

It wasn't mournful. It was a pretty uplifting show, mostly because Jai didn't play much. I was a bit disappointed, but I cheered up when Jai asked me to join him for a drink at the bar after the performance. He introduced me to some people who had gathered there. He didn't describe me as Miriam's friend. He introduced me simply as "a friend from Toronto." The people—acquaintances or friends, it was hard to tell—were all musicians of some sort and they were all trained in North Indian classical music. A couple of them played the tabla, some were vocalists, one was an older white guy who had a PhD in North Indian classical music from a university in India.

At one point, one of them asked what type of music I liked. "Do you like Hindustani music?" he said.

Hindustani music refers to North Indian classical music, which I knew. But for some reason I heard "Do you like Hindi music?" and I proceeded to name a few Hindi films I liked.

"Well, the songs," I clarified. "I like the songs." They all nodded in that way people do when you've said something stupid.

"Bollywood isn't so bad," one of them said. But no one agreed.

Suddenly Jai launched into them, told them all they were idiots. "Art is not something to be kept locked away for a small group of experts, for people who think they are better," Jai said. He said they were snobs who had no right to call themselves artists. He called them idiots once more, took a swig of beer, slammed his glass on the table, and walked away. Everyone was stunned into silence.

Without making eye contact with any of them, I stood up and headed for the exit, leaving my gin and tonic half finished.

When I stepped outside, Jai was standing next to the door, leaning against the wall. He apologized for his outburst but said, again, that those people were idiots.

"I got that," I said.

He smiled. Then he asked if Miriam was doing okay. I said she was.

"I love film songs," he said. "These people who think they are too pure are full of shit."

Now, I smiled. "It's okay," I said. "I've been around academics a lot, so I'm used to snobs. I'm a snob myself, about a lot of things."

He was looking at me as though I'd said something strange. It was a bit awkward, him just staring like that so I said good night and turned to head back to Miriam's. The bus stop was a good half kilometre away and it was getting late.

As I walked away, Jai started singing a verse from a Hindi film song, an old, famous one, a popular one. The lyrics are accusing. "You refuse to meet my eyes. You're afraid of the beating of your own heart."

I turned around; he was looking at me, still. Then he held his hand up, a signal to stop or a firm wave goodbye. I turned back and continued towards the bus stop. In my head, I finished the verse: *Even so, I'm determined to look at the ravaged flesh of my wounded heart.*

Chapter 19

I T OCCURS TO me I should tell you that about three months before I saw Miriam in Vancouver, I had walked out on my partner, Ben. The split was part of the reason I decided to apply for the teaching position at the University of Victoria (the other part was, as I mentioned, a final attempt at a career in academia). I needed to find a new place to live, in any case, and starting fresh on the other side of the country was appealing. Since moving out of Ben's house, I had been living in a colleague's basement apartment in Cabbagetown. It was a comfortable space, but I had to leave by year's end, when her mother was to move in.

By the time I told Ben I was leaving him, I'd already made arrangements to stay at my colleague's house. I'd even booked movers to come get my things (at a time when Ben was scheduled to be out of town). I didn't have a great deal to take with me. I had lived there only a year. As well, he had so much furniture in his house that I hadn't bothered to keep much of mine. (Most of it was pretty old or just cheap stuff from Ikea.) It was easy to leave in that way. I remember thinking, as I watched the movers fill up the smallest truck they had, *Thank goodness we never married*. Ben had been right about that, after all. It saved quite a bit of money, avoiding lawyers and all that, which should have pleased him.

Of course, Ben wasn't pleased; he was shocked. He didn't understand why we couldn't talk about it and fix whatever it was that wasn't working. I didn't tell him that I didn't love him anymore. Instead, I told him I didn't think our myriad problems could be fixed and, anyways, I'd lost the will to try. This was true.

My mother wasn't surprised. But she was disappointed. "I want you to be happy, have children, all the joys of this."

"I want that too," I said. "That's why I'm leaving."

"Maybe you leave, again and again, because I couldn't leave."

Thinking on it now, she can't have said that because I didn't leave again and again. Ben is the only man I have ever lived with and I left him only once. She said this during a somewhat confusing conversation, so it's possible I'm mistaken. We had been talking on the telephone, discussing Miriam and Jai (I didn't tell her about Peter or the pregnancy, only that they were in a "rough patch"), and Hassan Uncle came up. I told my mother what Miriam had reported to me about her father's health.

Hassan Uncle had experienced a number of medical crises over the last three or four years. It started with a heart attack, followed by a series of small strokes. Most recently—and this is what I was sharing with my mother—he had gangrene in his foot (a complication of the diabetes he had developed some decades earlier), which he ignored initially. When it was finally addressed, he had to have his leg amputated, just above the knee. He was living in Mbarara and travelled to Johannesburg for the surgery. Miriam would send me updates about Hassan Uncle's health here and there, usually in a letter but sometimes on the telephone. She told me about the amputation over the phone. It was at the end of a long conversation and she mentioned it as an afterthought.

"The doctors cut my dad's leg off," she said, or something equally blunt. It was startling and it took me a few seconds to respond. It struck me after that call how disconnected Miriam had become from her father. He no longer evoked any emotion in her whatsoever. I was sharing these thoughts with my mother when she interrupted me.

"How does Hassan pay to fly to Johannesburg for medical care?" she asked.

I didn't know. Miriam hadn't mentioned anything about his finances and I didn't think to ask.

"He left his daughter," my mother said. "He abandoned his only living child. I said it, didn't I? Leigh Ann finished him, as I always said she would."

I was stunned. My mother had not mentioned Leigh Ann to me in decades. The last time she even alluded to her was the day after Salim's funeral, when she was angry with my father for helping Leigh Ann terminate her pregnancy.

I misremembered.

All these years I had thought my mother said, "What kind of a woman asks a man for help with an abortion." But she hadn't. As I recalled the argument that day, I realized she had in fact said this: "When does a woman ask a man for help with an abortion?"

"Was Leigh Ann pregnant with Papa's child?" I asked my mother.

She was quiet for a few moments. Then she sighed. "I thought so," she said. "For years I was sure of it. But now, who knows? Papa used to say the baby would be Salim's before his, before even Hassan's."

"Why would he say that?"

"I don't know," she said. "I don't care. They disgust me. These men. They couldn't even trust each other. Hassan and Papa, and then bringing in that poor boy's name? I don't know."

"If you aren't sure that it was his baby—that he had an affair with her—it's good you didn't leave him back then," I said, "when you were planning to divorce him."

"I wasn't divorcing him because I was certain the

baby was his. I was divorcing him because I finally accepted that I could never trust him. Our marriage was finished long before Leigh Ann."

"But then he got sick," I said.

"Yes. I said to myself: *No one will look after him if I don't. What choice do I have but to stay?* Excuses. These were excuses," she said. "I couldn't leave. I didn't have the strength to leave."

That's when she asked me if I was leaving again and again because she couldn't.

Hassan Uncle died less than a month after Miriam and Zara did. My mother phoned to tell me she heard the announcement of his passing in jamat khana. "Good," she said. "He's gone now." After a few moments she added, "Poor man."

This isn't what I intended to talk about. I wanted to tell you about my decision to end my relationship with Ben.

Ben used to keep a ledger of expenditures. Whenever he updated it, he would ask what I'd spent on this or that. I had my own money, my own bank account, and I paid him rent to cover half of the mortgage. We had a joint account for utilities and groceries and gifts for our friends and things like that. It wasn't completely clear what was to be included in that list and, to be honest, I used it for lots of things without thinking too much about it. Afterwards I would pay Ben back. When he was updating his ledger (he did this twice a month), he would ask me about particular withdrawals. He did this usually by shouting because I was rarely in the room with him. He liked to sort out banking things in his home office rather than, say, the living room or kitchen. The problem is Ben had an accusing tone when he asked me these questions, as though he were angry with me for having spent money. But looking back, maybe I interpreted the shouting as anger when in fact it was simply a matter of needing to raise his voice to be heard from another room. For him—as for most of us—money brought a lot of stress, so he would hardly sound as though he were enjoying himself, would he? But I am considering all this only now. Back then I hated it when he asked me about my spending. I'd feel this burning sensation in my chest and throat, and I felt the urge to leave him, right then and there. His kids used to come stay with us two weekends a month (and on some weekdays) and he'd lavish money on them (then complain about the expense later). He also paid child support and alimony. Money was very tight for Ben. I knew this. But, also, I felt it was his problem. Not mine.

This reminds me of something that happened when I was ten, something, I think, that relates to my feelings around money and Ben. At that age, I had outgrown my purple bike, the one with the banana seat, on which I had learned to ride. Everyone at school had ten-speeds by then. My best friend at school, Jenny, had a beautiful blue Sekine bike. I didn't know anything about bicycles or if this was a good brand, but she kept going on about hers so I decided that it must be the best bicycle you could buy. She not only went on about how great her bike was, she also made fun of how ridiculous mine was, with its high handlebars and the fact it was far too small for me. I must have been begging my parents for a new bike, because one afternoon my father brought home a pickup truck from his garage and he loaded up our old bikes (mine and Saif's) to trade in for new ones. We drove to McPhail's Cycle Shop in Waterloo. I don't recall Saif coming with us, though he must have been there.

A salesman had a conversation with my father and then wheeled out a blue Sekine ten-speed (identical to the one that Jenny had). When I sat on it, it was perfect. The seat was soft but felt solid under my weight. The height was exactly right. I imagined I could go anywhere and do anything on this bike (the best, I had deemed, that money could buy). I couldn't wait to show Jenny. The sales guy seemed happy that I was happy, and he declared, "She looks great on it!"

Then my father asked the price. I don't remember what it cost but whatever the figure was it sent my father into a rage. "A bicycle costs this much?" he asked. "Really? For a child?"

He went on and on about how outrageous it was to charge this much for a bicycle, making a pretty awful scene. I remember the salesman standing there, saying nothing as I got off the bike and let him take it away. I have no memory of looking at cheaper bikes or talking any more at all to the salesman or anyone else in the shop. Nor do I recall getting back in the truck and going home. But obviously we did that.

A couple of weeks later my mother found a much cheaper bicycle in the Consumer's Distributing catalogue. It was a good, nice-looking ten-speed. It was silver-coloured and a fine bike. I rode it with Jenny and she even said it was a nice bike and didn't make fun of me anymore. But I didn't love it. To be honest, I didn't even like it. It took me places I wanted to go, but I didn't feel proud or happy riding on it. At school, I'd lock it at the end of the bike rack in a spot where you couldn't see it very well, tucked in behind another bike. Sometimes when I sat on it or looked at it for a bit, I would see in my mind the blue Sekine, the special bike on which I had no right to sit. Then I hated my silver ten-speed.

I realized that when Ben would ask me about my spending or when he'd complain about the bill in a restaurant after we finished dinner or the cost of the bottle of wine I wanted, I had the same feeling I had that day at McPhail's Cycle Shop and that came as residue sometimes when I sat on my silver ten-speed. What was the feeling? It wasn't quite embarrassment. I think it was shame. I was ashamed. An accusing voice was hollering in my head: *Who do you think you are? How dare you want this? How dare you think you have a right to it?*

The other thing that happened with Ben—and I think it was connected to what I just described—is that I wanted to have a baby. Ben was supportive. He was older than me but not yet fifty. "I would love to have a child with you," he had said when we were dating. About six months after I moved in with him, I went off the birth control pill, but I wasn't getting pregnant.

"I'm not sure what the issue is," I said one day after it had been about three months of trying (which isn't, I realized later, very long at all). "I'm perfectly fertile."

"What do you mean? Are you hoping to get pregnant?"

He didn't recall us having a conversation about trying to have a baby. He was fine with it, he said—we had discussed children before I moved in, which he recalled—but he genuinely couldn't remember talking about us actively starting to try.

After this I didn't speak to him for a few days. Maybe it was a bit childish on my part. But in my defence, I was feeling emotional because I didn't conceive immediately, which is what he said his wife had done with both her pregnancies.

"But did you?" Miriam asked when we were talking on the phone during that time. "Did you actually have a clear conversation about trying to get pregnant?"

"I can't believe you're taking his side," I said. "He obviously wasn't paying attention when we talked about it."

"I'm not taking his side. But he has had to deal with custody and child support, so I feel like he would want to be clear about more children. Maybe," she said, "you don't feel like you have the right to have a baby. And, so, you weren't clear with him."

"Like maybe I hedged?"

"Yes," she said. "Or you tried to slip it in because you were afraid he'd balk."

"Maybe," I said. "It's not easy, with his kids and his ex and everything."

"I know."

"I hate that my choices are limited by his past choices," I said, starting to feel sorry for myself.

"Are they?" she asked.

"What do you mean?" I was angry. "Of course, they are."

"It's your life. Do what you want," she said, stressing the *you*. "But first you have to know what you want. You don't need permission for any of it. Don't you get that? You need to get that."

Is that how she said it? *You need to get that.* It seems such odd phrasing for Miriam. But that's what I recall.

One day not long after this, Ben sent me an email with an Excel file attached. It was a list of what I owed him. "I'll keep it updated," he said. "This way I don't have to keep shouting down the hallway."

This was when my love for him evaporated. After that he disgusted me. Even the thought of him disgusted me. Looking back, of course I wasn't being fair. This is what we agreed to, financially. And he was being considerate of my feelings by avoiding the awkward conversations when he asked what I'd spent on things. But when I looked at that Excel file, which itemized things like highlights for my hair or a pair of jeans or some Thai food I had for lunch, I was enraged. I resented the cheques that went to his wife. I resented the fact of his entire previous family and how its existence meant that he had nothing left for me. With my teaching position at a private school for girls, I was bringing in a steady income. I could afford to pay him what I owed. He owned the house, but in the end, after his expenses, I had more disposable income than he did. Still, I resented that he didn't support me. I went back on the birth control pill.

I had a dream around that time. I was driving on what looked like the 401 or some other major highway that had loads of cars and trucks going very quickly. It was dark and snowing and I had to pay close attention to avoid an accident. Pretty soon, I lost control and swerved into a ditch. But I was comfortable there in the ditch. It was like a bed, all soft and warm, and so I relaxed and fell asleep, but then I woke up on the 401 again, driving in the snow and heavy traffic, and so I swerved on purpose and was back in the comfortable ditch. Again, I relaxed into sleep and awoke back on the 401, so I purposely swerved again into the ditch and fell into a sweet sleep, only to awake on the 401 yet again. It kept happening until I actually woke up. I told Miriam about the dream.

"Maybe I'm remembering Salim or something," I said.

"Possibly," she said. "But it seems like your unconscious mind is telling you that you keep choosing to be safe and hurt," she said. "You like feeling safe and hurt."

"But I'm not hurt in the dream. I'm so comfortable that I can't help but fall asleep. It's easier to be in there than on the highway."

"Okay then safe and asleep," she said. "Safe and unconscious."

I decided my life with Ben was the ditch.

"I'm not sure that's the way I'd interpret it," Miriam said.

"Well," I said, "it's my dream."

Chapter 20

MY MOTHER'S COMMENTS about leaving, about why I leave relationships, has got me thinking about something. Miriam told me, in bits and pieces when we were adults, how unhappy Begum had been during Miriam's childhood, even before Salim's death. Each time Hassan Uncle would have a girlfriend—a serious one or even just a date that Begum heard about from her children, from my parents, even from people in jamat khana—she would fall into a deep depression. According to Miriam, this involved a great deal of sobbing and the cursing of her existence for days or, sometimes, weeks at a time. She behaved as though her husband were cheating on her and humiliating her (when in fact she'd been divorced for years). In a sense—Miriam said this to me once though I can't remember exactly where or when—her mother never emotionally divorced her father. I'm realizing only now how profound an impact this had on Miriam.

Things became worse when Begum remarried, both for her and for Miriam.

When Miriam started high school (and I was in seventh grade), Hassan Uncle moved to Uganda to live full time. Miriam no longer had a reason to come to Kitchener, and for about six years we didn't lay eyes on each other. But because we exchanged letters regularly, it didn't feel as though we were separated all that long. Looking back, that period was in many ways the closest I've felt to Miriam. At the time I believed she was sharing everything with me: stories of cute boys at school, how this or that teacher had it in for her, things her school friends were doing that annoyed her. In turn I told her about my frustration with various basketball coaches, my latest crush, what I hoped my room would look like if my parents would ever let me redecorate it. Because we wrote each other so often we had trouble filling entire letters with these banal updates. Yet we both felt compelled to write a letter a couple of times a month or so. What this meant is that we discussed pretty much everything. For example, Miriam was excited about the first space shuttle mission, which took up a few letters. I remember we talked a lot about Charles and Diana's wedding. Movies and television were hot topics in our letters, as they'd been throughout our childhood. By the time I was in the ninth grade, I was telling Miriam about books I was reading. This was the point in my life when I began to engage, in a meaningful way, with literature.

One of my high school English teachers used to keep a pile of paperbacks in the back of the classroom; when you were done whatever work was assigned, you could go back and pick one to read. She let you take the books home as well. The first book that I remember reading from that pile was Margaret Laurence's novel *A Jest of God*. But the edition I read (released after the movie version) was called *Rachel, Rachel*. On the cover of this edition was an illustration of a naked man and woman (from the waist up; it wasn't pornographic or anything) embracing. I read the book fairly quickly and didn't dislike it, but I felt it was perhaps meant for a different reader, maybe an older woman. A few weeks later, I discovered an earlier edition—in the same pile at the back of the classroom—with the original title, which was, as I say, *A Jest of God*. Though the blurb on the back was similar, I thought this might be a slightly different book, so I took it home for the weekend. It quickly became clear it was the same book. But I had nothing else to read, so I finished it.

"The book changed with the title," I wrote to Miriam. "*Rachel, Rachel* was like one of those R-rated movies about lonely women. But when I read it as *A Jest of God*, there was more there. Like this woman, Rachel, seems to be trapped, forced to look after her elderly, annoying mother, but really she's trapping herself. She's hiding. When the book was called *A Jest of God*, I felt like the author must be talking about big stuff. It must be there somewhere in the book, so I looked for it. And I found it. I really liked it."

"The book didn't change, though," she wrote back. "The words were exactly the same (you told me), so you didn't find something in the book that hadn't been there before. That's impossible. You had to have found it in yourself."

While I had taken to sharing my thoughts about literature, Miriam drew pictures. Initially these were little doodles she made throughout the letters, but eventually she drew cartoon figures of people and asked me to guess who they were. She drew Spock and Fat Albert and Michael Jackson and other TV characters or famous people with distinctive appearances. Then she moved to family. They were pretty simple renditions, but I was impressed with the details she would add to provide hints about who she'd drawn. For example, when she drew my mother, she included the gold bangles she always wore on her right wrist. Or the Saif she depicted had a scar on his chin from a bad fall he had when he was a toddler.

Once, she drew a fat guy with two hairs poking out of his otherwise bald oval head and eyebrows turned inward so he looked angry all the time.

I couldn't guess this one and so Miriam added a speech bubble. "I am a brilliant doctor," the man said. "Doctors are gods. You must all obey me." Still, I didn't know. In the next letter, she added another speech bubble and then I guessed it. "I have found a wife to obey me. Oh no, she has a horrible, disobedient daughter. What to do?"

Miriam's stepfather, Zulfikar, was a doctor. Everyone called him Julie (which in Gujarati is a diminutive of Zulfikar). Miriam, at least in the cartoon version, called him Fathead. It occurs to me just now that I never did know how she addressed him. In any case, in Miriam's drawings, Fathead was a very cheap man and as a result would find himself in messes because he would try (and fail) to get out of paying for hotels or for dinners at restaurants. Miriam wouldn't draw him at hotels or restaurants or anywhere else for that matter. Her drawings were rudimentary. We would see Fathead, in his stick-figure form, with a speech bubble over his head, relating his experiences to his wife, whom he called Dingbat, and who would be shown, always, from behind. Miriam drew a stick-figure wearing a dress with a round black bun on her head. She would just stand there. She never spoke. I never saw a bubble over the wife's head. She was basically decoration or (as I sorted out later when I had the vocabulary and literary understanding) a narrative device that allowed Fathead to tell his story.

Miriam began to draw frames around each scene, like a comic strip. Eventually she stacked these strips on a whole page so that it looked like an actual comic book. She didn't colour them in or anything; they really did remain simple stick figures with speech bubbles, but they were engaging and entertaining. She ended each letter with a cliffhanger. "Will Fathead be thrown out of the dim sum place? Find out Next Time!"

I don't know at what point this happened but—for a time—Miriam completely stopped writing proper letters. She only sent me the comics she created. By this time I had stopped writing back to her because she wasn't responding to my letters, even when I asked her specific questions about poems or books. I wasn't especially offended by this. I enjoyed reading her comic books. They always featured Fathead but, after a month or so, another main character appeared. Gloria was, like the other characters, a stick figure, but she had flowing hair and a pair of perfectly round boobs. Clearly, Miriam was playing off the characters from the television show *All in the Family*. But apart from some of the characters' names, her comics bore little resemblance to the program. Miriam's Gloria would do things like put crumbs in Fathead's bed so he couldn't sleep. She would use a key to make tiny little scratches on his Mercedes that he wouldn't notice for a long, long time.

Fathead sometimes called Gloria "Goil" or "Little Goil," but mostly he called her "Whoria." Or "Slut." Gloria called him "Fathead" or "Loser." It was all extraordinarily silly, and it made me laugh. I'd look forward to each letter. The storyline always went like this: Fathead, who was cheap and fairly stupid, called Gloria mean names. In response, Gloria would do things to annoy him. Though he'd come tantalizingly close, he would never catch her in the act.

After about three or four months, Miriam abruptly stopped sending me the comic books, with no real resolution to the travails of Fathead and Gloria. I suppose she became bored. I have to admit I was growing a bit tired of the repetitive stories as well. After this, we resumed sending each other regular letters, but not nearly as often. Years later, when Miriam was visiting me and Ben, Ben's younger son—who was eight or so at that time—was drawing some stick figures on a small blackboard we had in the kitchen. I mentioned that Miriam was an expert and brought up her comic books, but her recollection was different from mine.

"Didn't I just draw stick people a few times?" she asked.

"No, you did a lot of them, entire comic books, and for a long time."

"Wow," she said. "I have no memory of this."

It's not surprising—considering what I learned later—that Miriam blocked out much of her life with Julie.

When Miriam was in grade eleven, Begum and Julie divorced. Miriam announced it by sending an envelope filled only with confetti (little pieces of paper that she had ripped up). A few weeks later, she told me she was deliriously happy living in a cramped little apartment with Begum. I knew, because Miriam had told me years earlier, that Hassan Uncle hadn't been paying child support for a long time. And, so, Miriam took a part-time job working in the dining room of the seniors' home where Begum was employed. She decided to take a year off after high school to work full time to save up some money for university.

I asked her if she was disappointed about losing a year.

"We don't have grade thirteen in BC, so I have one less year of high school than I thought I'd have. Also," she added, "I'd work digging ditches for the rest of my life if it meant I didn't have to live with that asshole."

Eight years after divorcing Julie, Begum died of heart issues that had plagued her for a number of years. Later that same year, Julie was stripped of his medical licence for sexually abusing four of his female patients. "He was found to be doing examinations that were not clinically warranted," Miriam told me over the phone. "That's what the official ruling is."

As shocked as I was by these charges, I was almost as shocked at Miriam's nonchalant way of talking about it.

"Because it's not surprising," she said.

"What do you mean?" I asked. "Did you have some idea? Was he a creep with you?"

"He didn't touch me or anything. But he is a pig. An entitled pig. He uses his money and social power to make you feel small and powerless. He gets off on it. I'm a doctor, blah blah blah, how dare so and so talk to me like that.

"I used to envy you," Miriam said, "with two parents, a normal family. Until him. After him, all I wanted was to go back to living in our sweet little dump at Banting Place."

A few years later, when Miriam had come to Toronto for the party my mother threw for Ben and me, she and I went out to a Chinese restaurant near Kensington Market, not far from a basement apartment I used to rent when I was a student. It was nighttime and the lights in the restaurant were bright, unpleasantly bright, and Miriam's face had this sheen on it, like she had been sweating. I had been complaining about Ben's ex-wife who seemed to be dropping by more often at that time, on some pretext or other. I said something about how I wished she'd move on from her marriage to Ben, when Miriam said this: "I told Begum if she didn't leave Julie, I'd kill myself. I said, if I have to keep living in this house with this man, I'm going to fall into a hell I can't get out from. That did it. She left him after that."

We hadn't spoken about Julie since she shared the news of his licence being revoked, or if we had I had no memory of it. "Why didn't you tell me any of this," I asked, "before now?"

She shrugged. "I guess I wanted to put it behind me. Or pretend it never happened. But I can't. I can't put it behind me." I watched her sip her Coke as I picked at a plate of prawns mixed with green beans. I remember my meal clearly because I was staring at my plate when Miriam told me that Julie used to slap and punch her mother and if Miriam tried to intervene, he'd scream abuse at her, calling her a whore and a slut.

"Did he hit you?" I asked.

She shook her head. "They would fight a lot at the beginning. Yelling and all that, which—seriously—I thought was a fairly normal marriage. But one night it was different. I don't know what woke me up. But I went into the hallway and Begum was cowering on the floor in the corner. I saw him standing nearby; I was between them at this point, and he had this look on his face like he was possessed. His face was dark, actually darker in shade. Like a shadow was over it. Then I looked closely at her down there on the floor. The lights were on, so it should have been obvious. But it was like my brain couldn't process right away that her face, on one side, was swelling up. And I think I said, 'Did you hit her?' I don't remember exactly. He said his 'disgusting whore' thing or whatever to me but then he stepped towards me, like he was lunging at me. I got scared. He was like a cornered animal. I backed right away. I thought, *This guy is going to kill me.* Begum slept in my room that night and we locked the door. That was the first time he hit her, or the first time I knew he hit her.

"The next morning, he had gone out early and bought pastries and flowers, and he brought her an ice pack and even some medication to make her feel better. He doted on her. Over the next days and weeks, he bought her gold bangles and a diamond ring and treated her like a queen, like no one has treated her in her life. He even bought me a stereo for my room and gave me cash every couple of days 'to do something fun.' For weeks, even months, he was this super husband and dad. I felt crazy. Completely crazy because I was trying in the midst of that to convince Begum to leave him. But then he did it again. He hit her again.

"She wouldn't leave though. Once, I tried to physic-ally drag her out of the house. But she started screaming and freaking out and I thought I was abusing her too. I didn't know what to do. What do you do? Do you call the police and say, 'My mom won't leave?' What do I do? Who do I call?"

"God, Miriam."

"But you know what was really insane? He would choke her. He would put his hands on her throat and strangle her. I never saw him do it. She denied it. But he did it. And that's not the insane part. This is the insane part: She'd have black eyes and burst blood vessels in the whites of her eyes and her voice would be hoarse because he almost fucking killed her, and she'd say, 'I will be better, then he will be better.' I would sob and she wouldn't care. I'd beg her to leave before he killed her, and she just walked out of the room. Until I said I would kill myself. That's when she snapped out of it, for a time, long enough to leave. After that she was angry as all hell at me. For years she said, 'Because of you I left. Because of you I will die alone. Because of you I'm nothing.' She said it even in the days before she died. 'Because of you I have no husband. I am nothing.'"

AFTER MIRIAM DIED, I looked for those letters, the ones with the comic strips. I knew I had them. I'd kept them move after move in one of those portable filing cases, the accordion kind. I found the filing case and I found the letters, a pile of them, maybe ten or so. I pulled them out and sat down to read. Many of the letters were stuck to each other, and when I pulled them apart, I saw that the ink had faded. You could make out the first few words and lines at the tops of the letters and some pen marks on the sides a bit, but the rest of the pages were blank. It was as though someone had wiped them clean.

Chapter 21

C AT WASN'T SUPPOSED to be there. Miriam assured me she had taken the children to visit her parents for a few days. Peter was travelling, as well, for work. Miriam had insisted I go and see their house while I was in Victoria for my job interview. "You're planning to go for a drive by the ocean, so why not stop by?" she had said. "It's in a place called Oak Bay, which is not far from the university. The house is stunning. I know you love fabulous houses." My love of fabulous houses consisted, in those days, of me watching renovation and real estate shows on television. I suppose I did tend to go on a bit about these shows to Miriam so maybe she thought I was more interested than I was. But still I found it strange that she insisted I go look at Peter's house. It's probably more accurate, now that I know what I know about it, to call it Cat and Peter's house. He had built it for her. Later, after Cat died, Miriam told me this, and added with a hint of disgust, "Cat called it her Taj Mahal."

This reminds me of how when we were kids, Miriam—who I've said before had little interest in most Indian things—was nevertheless slightly obsessed with a miniature marble Taj Mahal souvenir, or rather she was obsessed with the memory of it. According to Miriam, this little statue used to sit on a side table in the house in Mbarara where she lived with Salim and their parents, who were still married at the time. She talked quite a lot about this statue during our childhood. Sometimes when we were particularly bored and she started doodling or something, she would draw it. She said it was cold and heavy and she loved to hold it in her hands and imagine little people living inside, a tiny Miriam and tiny Salim and their tiny parents. She wasn't allowed to play with it because it wasn't a toy, but she would do so when her parents weren't looking. I found all this hard to believe. Miriam wasn't even four when her parents divorced. I doubted she could remember this much detail from the time before that. And even if she could, how in the world was she sneaking off with a little marble statue when she was hardly more than a toddler?

When I was going on my backpacking tour of India she asked me to bring back one of these Taj Mahal souvenirs. She had yet to find one anywhere. Until she said this, I had no idea she had even been looking for one. "I'll pay you back," she said. "But please pick it up if you see it."

Of course, when I was in India I made the journey to Agra to see the Taj Mahal, as most tourists do. (I'm sure you know the story of this architectural wonder. It was commissioned in the seventeenth century by the Mughal emperor Shah Jahan as a mausoleum for his favourite wife, Mumtaz.) When I arrived at the Taj Mahal, there was a set of enormous doors that led to the entrance of the grounds. Vendors selling souvenirs and food and whatnot gathered in the area in front of these doors and it was here that I found Miriam's marble Taj Mahal souvenir. A boy, who looked to be about ten or eleven, was hollering in English, astonishingly with an American accent, the merits of buying his miniature Taj Mahal. He was by no means the only vendor selling these, but his accent and his exuberance attracted me, and I wandered over to him. As it turns out, his English was very limited; he had memorized the phrases he was shouting. In response to my question in Hindi, he explained—also in Hindi—that he had learned to speak English from tourists.

After our transaction he smiled and pointed at the miniature Taj Mahal I was holding, and which he had just sold me for far more than it was worth. "This will bring you luck," he said, using one of his memorized English phrases. It's equally possible he said love. "This will bring you love."

When I gave it to Miriam, I shared this exchange and the two possible interpretations of the boy's parting message. We laughed and she thanked me profusely. "It's exactly like the one we had," she said, "when I was little." It occurs to me I'd never heard Miriam refer to her birth family as "we," before or since.

A few hours later, when I was leaving—I had been at Miriam's apartment, the one she shared with her first husband, to drop off her gift—she said something strange. At this point we hadn't discussed the souvenir for quite a while. But she said, as I was stepping off her porch, "I know everyone says the Taj Mahal is a monument to love, but I've always thought it's a monument to loss." She laughed, nervously. I remember this little laugh because it was so out of character for Miriam. "Maybe it's the same thing," she said.

"Maybe," I said. I was in a rush for some reason, though I can't recall where I needed to be. I do know it was a thoughtless response on my part because now that I think of it, it's not. It's not the same thing.

Miriam very badly wanted me to see Cat's Taj Mahal. I think sending me there was her way of claiming it for herself. Peter designed the house with all the features Cat wanted, including the high ceilings and the enormous windows overlooking the ocean. She also requested an art studio with lots of natural light, and a big indoor playroom for the children, equipped with a swing. An oversized black-and-white print of Cat and Peter from their wedding day was mounted on the living room wall, a surprise from Peter to his wife on some anniversary, apparently. Apart from that photograph, Cat selected all the decor, and her artwork—which, as you might recall, Miriam detested—graced the walls. All this to say, after Cat died, Miriam moved into an actual monument to the life Peter and Cat shared.

I should mention here that neither Peter nor Cat gave Miriam this information (about the house being her Taj Mahal or that Peter designed it to her specifications). Miriam read all of this in Cat's journals, which she found tucked in behind the brushes in her art studio. Miriam became pretty obsessed with those journals.

"It's unhealthy," I said more than once. "Stop reading them."

Miriam didn't stop; she started to read me snippets over the phone. Then one day she declared that she was going to burn the journals.

"Why?" I asked.

"Why not?"

"They aren't yours."

"Whose are they?" Miriam asked. "Cat has no use for them anymore. It's clear from what's in them she never wanted Peter to read them."

"Leave them for her kids or family," I said. "Doesn't she have a sister?"

"No. She's an only child. Listen, she writes about her sexual urges, among other things, including what a whore I am. Who wants to read this about their mother? Or their daughter? I would rather die than know Begum's secrets. If I kept a journal, I would like it burned after I die."

"Still," I said. "I don't think it's right for you to destroy them. The boys are what? Four and five? Maybe years from now they will want to read about their mother's thoughts, even the terrible ones."

"I know things about Cat that Peter doesn't know," she said, ignoring what I'd said. "Isn't that crazy? I know her innermost thoughts. Her deep, dark desires."

It hit me suddenly right then why Miriam wanted to burn the journals. She was trying to destroy Cat's presence in their lives and this was a tangible way to do it. That's when I suggested they all move out of that house so they could build their own life.

"That's the plan," Miriam said. "But not yet. Peter wants to give the boys some more time."

"Time for what?"

"Their mother died, and this is the only house they've known."

"But she died a year ago," I said. "They were practically babies then. It's better to make the move when they're young. Don't you think?"

"I don't know," Miriam said, irritably. "It doesn't matter what I think. I can't force him."

It was pretty shocking to hear Miriam talk like this, as though her life were no longer in her control. It made me a bit frustrated, to be honest. "Leave," I said. "Take Zara and leave."

"Why?" she said. "Why would I leave? He's a good father. He's thinking about his kids."

"What about Zara?" I said. "She's his kid too. Is it fair for her mother to live in this insane situation—"

"What are you talking about? What insane situation?"

"Miriam, you aren't working. I mean, for God's sake, all that new research you started about dark energy and—boom—you stopped cold. And now? You're sleeping in their marital bed. You told me you use her coffee mug and those bowls she made in ceramics class—"

"It's just some dishes and shit," she said. "You romanticize everything. You manufacture all this drama around things. It's just stuff. What are we going to do? Throw it all away? And listen to you, anyway. What are you doing with your life? How sane is your situation? Let's talk about work. What happened to the books you were going to write? First you spend years getting a doctorate to avoid saying a damn thing yourself and now you spend your days standing in front of a class of spoiled teenagers whose tuition is as high as your salary, trying to convince them not to hate poetry." She wasn't finished. "Oh, and you dump a guy because he's not some prince in a fairy tale. Where do you get off judging me?"

Before I could respond, before I could even absorb what she had said, she said this: "Listen to me, Peter loves Zara. He loves her. That's why we aren't going anywhere. This is her family. This is my family."

Then she hung up. She apologized eventually, maybe later that night or the next, saying she realized that I had only been trying to help but that she and Peter would figure out their living arrangements themselves. I honestly don't remember the details of that call.

Eventually Miriam and Zara moved out of Cat's Taj Mahal, but Peter never did. As far as I know he still lives there. At some point, I'm not sure when because she told me long after the fact, Miriam burned Cat's journals. All of them. Even the ones from Cat's childhood, when she was a thirteen-year-old schoolgirl writing about her crush on Leif Garrett.

But all of this came later. I need to back up and tell you about the morning in Victoria when I ran into Cat. It was three days after I'd visited Miriam in Vancouver. When she first suggested I go see the house, I refused. It seemed macabre or something, like I was a vulture picking at the carcass of her lover's old life. But she insisted no one would be there and that it was a beautiful house on a beautiful road. I finally said I'd consider it just so she would shut up. I had no intention of going, but on the day of the interview I woke up at five a.m., still on Ontario time, and I couldn't go back to sleep. My interview wasn't until late that afternoon, so I bought a cup of coffee, got into my rental car, and followed the directions Miriam had written down for me.

She was right. It was a beautiful road, particularly as the sun was coming up.

To reach Peter and Cat's house, to actually see it, you have to go along a winding driveway. When I arrived at the house, I saw someone standing next to a flower bed. Based on Miriam's description of her—tall, auburn hair—I guessed it was Cat. I could have turned the car around at this point and driven away. I've replayed this moment in my mind so many times. And each time I replay it, I do exactly that. I turn around and continue my pretty drive, maybe buy some breakfast at a café, and then ace the interview and carry on with my life. But this isn't what I did. What I did is I stopped the engine, opened the door, stepped out, and walked towards Cat. I did this intentionally, as though I had driven here for the sole purpose of talking to her. To this day, I don't know what propelled me.

"Can I help you?" she said, backing up slightly as I came closer.

I didn't want to scare her, so I stopped and smiled. "Are you Catherine?" I asked. I was close enough to her, about a metre away, to be able to discern small movements. I noticed her body stiffen.

"Yes?" She said it with an inflection at the end, as though it were a question.

"I'm a friend of Miriam's."

The colour drained from her face.

"I think you should know something," I said, before she could respond. I want to say I stammered or paused. But I didn't. The words came without hesitation, clearly, pretty loudly. "Miriam is pregnant with Peter's baby."

Now her face became bright pink. I remember thinking how maddening it must be to be so pale skinned that you unwittingly telegraph your emotions like this. Her lip curled and then she laughed. "She dispatched her friend to tell me?"

"No," I said. "Not at all. She didn't know you would be here. I wanted to see the house. I like beautiful houses. I happened to be in Victoria for work and I had some time to kill. I had no idea you would be here. But now that you are, I've told you. It's good you know."

"What a strange friend you are."

"I just think people should know the truth," I said, "so they can make informed choices."

"Ahhh," she said, dragging the word out like she'd figured me out or caught me or something. It really annoyed me and I hated her in that moment. "I understand now," she said. "You want me out of the picture. So your friend can move into this house you just had to see?"

"To be honest," I said, "it was my understanding you were already out of the picture."

She didn't move. The expression that settled on her face terrified me. I'm not sure what I was afraid of, her screaming at me or actually physically attacking me. I turned around, walked back to the car, got in, started the engine, and did a three-point turn all without looking at her. As I eased down the driveway, I glanced in the rear-view mirror. Cat was sitting on the steps leading up to her porch, her face buried in her hands.

Chapter 22

LOOKING BACK, I suppose Cat was right. I was helping Miriam by telling Cat about the baby. Miriam wanted a family with Peter and he didn't appear to be in any rush to divorce his wife. Now that Cat knew, she would divorce him. But I was helping Cat too. She had a right to know, didn't she? Regardless, I considered all this later. At the time I didn't think about my motivation for telling Cat that Miriam was pregnant. I wasn't thinking at all. I guess if I had to ascribe a motive to my actions in the moment, I'd say I wanted the truth out. People keeping secrets has always pissed me off.

As you can imagine, my job interview later that day, after my confrontation with Cat, didn't go well. I had trouble focusing on the questions being posed and, at times, I found myself picturing Cat sitting across the table glaring at me. As a result, my answers were mostly incoherent, even to my own ears. The thing is, my CV was weak; I hadn't published a research paper in years. But because this was a lecturer position, I knew I had a shot if I could impress them in the interview. Instead, I blew it. I wasn't officially rejected until a couple of weeks later, though. Before this—in fact, only hours after I arrived home in Toronto—I heard from Miriam.

"Why did you tell her?" Miriam said over the phone. "Of course, Peter thinks I put you up to it."

"You insisted I go there," I said. "You said she wouldn't be there."

"How does any of that have a thing to do with you telling her I'm pregnant with Peter's baby?"

"I don't know," I said. "She was there. She was standing there, just—it's like she was waiting for me. It was so weird. And then I blurted it out. I don't know—"

"Stop saying 'I don't know.' How do you not know?"

"What I'm saying is that I surprised myself. Really, Miriam, I didn't plan to say anything. I kind of blurted it."

She was quiet for a few moments. "Why didn't you tell me then, after the fact? After you blurted it to her why didn't you pick up the phone and tell me?"

"I didn't think it was that big a deal. Honestly, I never understood the secrecy. Wouldn't she notice you're pregnant? And even if you decided not to keep the baby, weren't you and Peter going to stay together? What is the point of hiding this from her? It's like he was protecting her and you were helping him. I mean, she is a grown woman."

"She freaked out," Miriam said. "She smashed things. She totally, completely smashed the wedding photos they had on the walls. Peter had to take her to the emergency room and they sedated her."

"Oh my God," I said.

"I wish you'd have shared your concerns about *our decision* not to tell her with me instead of telling her," Miriam said, and then added in a clipped voice, "Everything is a complete mess now."

"And you're blaming me?" I asked.

"You're the one who told her."

It felt as though my chest had caught on fire. Miriam had an affair with this woman's husband without—it appeared—bothering to use birth control; she first snuck around with him behind Cat's back and then hid a pregnancy from her, but somehow the fallout was my fault? I was so angry I hung up. In all our phone calls over all the years we knew each other, this is the only time I hung up on Miriam. I believed in that moment that I would never speak to her again.

A few days later Miriam called me. I saw her number on my telephone display and ignored it. But I stood next to the telephone and listened as she left a message: "I'm sorry. You were right. You were completely, totally right. It was fair to everyone to know. We can all move forward now. I'm sorry—"

I picked up the phone.

Peter and Cat had started divorce proceedings. It would be slow. Sorting out a separation agreement for the children would take time, as these things do. But the process had begun. Their marriage was effectively over.

"I guess I wanted Peter to be the one to tell her because it would prove to me that he wanted to end things. But it's hard. The kids are young and it's hard. He wouldn't be the first man to avoid doing something hard, would he?"

"So, I take it Cat is feeling better?" I asked. "The last time we talked, you said she needed to be sedated."

"Yes, she's fine, normal. She wants to settle the legal stuff as soon as possible. Peter is giving her the house outright, which is great news. I'm going to have my family," Miriam said. "My own family."

Because she had always been so insistent that she never wanted children, I never imagined this. Miriam as a mother, and with a brood no less. She told me that she and Peter were looking at real estate listings. I told her I was happy for her.

Two months later, Cat decided to go on a holiday with a few close friends. She wanted a break before the next chapter in her life. That's what she told Peter, who shared all of this with Miriam, who told me. Cat needed to go be with her friends, away from all the lawyers and the drama, and so they booked a trip at a resort in Puerto Vallarta. They stayed at a hotel near the Vancouver airport because the flight to Mexico was very early the next day. At some point before the sun came up, Cat went out for a walk. Someone—a man who worked for the hotel and was doing a repair or something—saw her fall into the river, but he was at a distance. The current was very swift, and by the time he reached the water's edge she was out of sight. Emergency services pulled her body out a few hours later.

"Why was she out there in the middle of the night, standing on the dock?" Miriam said. "Who does that? And how do you fall into the Fraser River? It's not a little lake next to rocks you could slip on."

However it happened, Cat's death ruined everything for Miriam.

There was no reason any longer to move out of the house, so Peter cancelled the showings they had with the real estate agent. Miriam remained—for a time—in the apartment in Vancouver (Jai had moved out). She and Peter both agreed it was the right thing to do. Miriam was starting to show and people—Cat's parents, Peter's parents—might guess she was expecting. It seemed unnecessary to showcase her pregnancy while their grief was fresh. She moved in a few weeks later, after the family members had all returned to their homes. We talked on the phone fairly often during that time, at least once a day.

"Our baby is growing in me, but it's like I'm shrinking in him," Miriam said in one of those conversations. "Cat is on his mind all the time. She's perfect. Their marriage was perfect. You should hear him go on about it. God."

"Of course, he'd say that," I said. "Death smooths everything over. You know their marriage wasn't perfect."

"Well, it's casting a perfectly massive shadow over me," she said.

The last time I saw Miriam was when Zara was two and a half or so. I had flown to Victoria and spent a weekend with her and the baby after she called and begged me to come. Peter was taking the boys camping. "I need a friend," she had said. "Please." Miriam had never asked me to come to her, ever. Even in the deepest of her Lows she had not asked me to come. It was a long way to go for only two days, and the last-minute flight wasn't cheap. But I couldn't say no.

I was a bit shocked when I saw her. She looked much older than the last time I had seen her, which was only three years earlier. She had put on weight—or she had held onto some of her pregnancy weight, I suppose—and she carried a lot of it in her jowls, so that they pulled down the sides of her mouth and made her appear sad or angry or both. I could tell she was colouring her hair in the sink. Miriam had started going gray in her mid-twenties and she would get her hair coloured at the salon. No matter how poor she was, she'd find a way, including having her hair done by hairdressing students. What I mean to say is, she always had beautiful highlights. Now her hair had that opaque look box colour gives.

Miriam was convinced Peter was sleeping with another architect at his firm, and she spent much of our weekend talking about this alleged affair, telling me how he was always working late, how he would have quiet conversations on the phone late in the night, how when Miriam had stopped by his office this woman had looked her up and down with the disdain of a soap opera villainess. Despite this, Miriam still hoped he'd marry her and that they would buy a new house. But he was stalling on both fronts. There were always reasons: the boys, his father, the real estate market, his work schedule.

After a few glasses of wine late one night, Miriam told me the real reason was Cat. The ghost of Cat. "She haunts us all," Miriam said. "Cat and I had a conversation after that lecture on stars. You remember I told you we went to that lecture? It was a stupid conversation. Cat didn't grasp anything of substance from the talk. Such a stupid conversation."

Miriam was lying on a sofa in the living room and I was sitting in an armchair across from her. I was jet lagged and so, unlike Miriam, had only had a few sips of wine. Because I was sober and she was not, her rambling was becoming a bit tiresome. But I could tell she needed to talk and so I stayed with her instead of heading to bed, which I desperately wanted to do.

"The conversation keeps replaying in my mind," she said. "I don't know why. Ever since she died, it plays on a loop. It's making me crazy."

"What did she say?" I asked.

"She said it like it was a triumph, like she won. 'Stars

can be so massive they collapse immediately into a singularity.'"

"She was talking about black holes?" I asked.

"Yes," Miriam said. "In the lecture they talked about black holes, and Cat seemed to think this proved she had been right to ascribe emotions to stellar activity. She said, 'See. It is sad when a star dies.' And I said, 'No. It isn't sad. Black holes aren't sad. They're part of the universe, an integral, central part of the universe.' For God's sake, this is my work; why is she arguing with me? 'It's sad because light can't penetrate,' she said. 'Light can't live in them.' 'No,' I said. 'This is not accurate. Black holes absorb light. Light can't escape a black hole. It's pulled in. Everything is pulled into a black hole. Even light. Even light.'"

And then Miriam told me about a game, the only game, Peter played with his daughter. He would give Zara a sip of beer. (She loved beer, Miriam explained to me with what I perceived was a hint of pride.) And then another. And another. Until she was swaying as she walked, unable to articulate even the few childish words she knew. Everyone would laugh. He would smile. He looked thoughtful in those moments. Loving.

"*Oh, how he loves his daughter despite the complicated situation, despite the split in him, demanded of him.* That's what I thought then," Miriam said. "Now," she said, looking at me, the circles under her eyes deep and dark, her jaw set, "I wonder if he ever made her children drunk to entertain his friends. I wonder if she sat there like an idiot and let him do it."

On the last day of my visit—a couple of hours before I was to leave—we were sitting on the deck of the house, which I suppose I should call Miriam's house but I cannot seem to do. The deck faced the ocean and the view was stunning. It was a warm fall day. The sea was calm after a windy few days; the sky was clear. Zara was in her bedroom, having her afternoon nap.

"Peter begged me to terminate the pregnancy," Miriam said. She said this quite suddenly. I can't recall what we had been talking about, but this did not follow what had come before, that much I remember because her words startled me. "He begged," she said. "He sobbed. 'This baby is the reason Cat died. She killed herself because of this baby.' Then he stopped crying and he commanded, 'I want it gone.' When he said that, I walked away. I left him. I went back to Jai. I told him I wanted to get back together. He had offered. He had offered to raise the baby as his. But that was before. Now he wouldn't. He said he couldn't. So, I scheduled an abortion and left a message for Peter that I was doing as he asked. He called me and begged me again, this time not to do it. He insisted he hadn't meant it. And he drove to pick me up and he said, 'Let's go home.' That's what he said. 'Let's go home.' I made it my home. Put some art up that I liked, bought a new sofa. I cleaned up after the boys and made them breakfast and washed all their dishes. I stood there while Cat's parents—who showed up unannounced when they heard I was living there—told me I was a piece of trash." She laughed now. "They actually said that, 'a piece of trash.' Peter comforted them because they were so upset and crying, and so I walked down to the water and sat on a rock, heavily pregnant, due any day, and waited until I saw their car drive off."

"Why did you stay?" I asked. "You could have raised Zara on your own. You didn't need him. Why didn't you leave? Why did you take all this crap?"

"He was nice after that. He thanked me for staying calm when they were yelling. He told me he loved me. Said we'd be okay. Talked about the beautiful family we'd have together. We already were a family. We are a family. Zara's not going to grow up the way I did. She has a family."

"He won't marry you," I said. "He's cheating; you said it yourself. This man is garbage. Leave. Come on, Miriam. You've left better men than Peter. Take Zara and go. I know money is an issue; you can come stay with me. We can manage until you find a postdoc or something. You're not trapped here. You have somewhere to go."

"What do you think?" she asked. "Do you think Jai and I could have been okay? Raised Zara together?"

I was confused. What did it matter now? "Probably," I said. "I don't know."

She stared at me, her eyes fixed on my face, until I asked her what was going on.

"You told Jai about that guy I slept with before the wedding. You told him I was a cheater and always would be. A whore."

"No," I said. "I didn't use that word. I never would."

"But a cheater. You said that. That's okay to say, and sharing a secret I told you—"

"It's true. You were," I said, "a cheater."

"I told myself he made it up," she said. "He was enraged. You wouldn't say those things. It was him. His anger. Not you. But you did."

I was quiet. I did say those things. I called Jai after hanging up on Miriam that day she blamed me for ruining everything by telling Cat she was pregnant. I went on and on. I told him about every time she had cheated. About how she never left a relationship without cheating. About how she toyed with men. I said she was selfish and cruel. But I didn't call her a whore.

"You told him how we laughed at him," Miriam said.

"I told him how you laughed at him. Not me. I never laughed at Jai."

She turned away from me to face the ocean.

"Come on, Miriam, it was ages ago. I was so angry."

"About what?" she said, her head snapping back to face me. "What did I do to you?"

"You take what you want. You always take what you want." The words came out with such force I surprised myself.

"What's wrong with taking what you want? Why is that bad?"

"You wrecked a whole family. You hurt people. You hurt Jai and Cat and the kids. I was angry that after all that, you were getting what you wanted. Everything you wanted. A whole family in a dream house in a dream life. Yet another man worshipping you. God, Miriam. After everything you did, why should you have it all? Why should you?"

She didn't say anything. Her body seemed to slump. But maybe she had already been sitting in this way and I only noticed it now. I noticed rolls in her midsection. I noticed her hair was greasy.

"Okay," she said, standing up, walking towards the house.

"Miriam—" But she kept walking. I followed her into the house, but she wouldn't talk to me. She kept staring straight ahead. No matter what I said, she ignored me. Even when I said I was sorry, so very sorry. Even when I said I was stupid and a horrible person and of course she deserves to be happy, she kept ignoring me, moving about, making a snack for Zara, tidying up, putting away dishes as though I were nothing. As though I were a ghost. Even when I got into a taxi a few hours later and waved and shouted through the window that I'd call her when I got home, she said nothing.

We never spoke again.

Chapter 23

JAI WAS THE one who called to tell me Miriam and
Zara had died. The service would be small and
Peter was choosing to keep it private, though of
course I would be welcome. I said I couldn't possibly
go; it was an unusually busy time at work. The truth
is, I was terrified to face Peter and his family. And I
could do nothing for Miriam anymore. Peter told Jai
he intended to have their ashes placed in a columbarium at a cemetery in Victoria and would forward the
information later. Jai assured me he would let me know
when he knew.

That was two years ago.

A few weeks ago, Jai was in Toronto performing with
his band, Dharm. By chance I saw an advertisement
for the performance online. I had been browsing the

internet and found myself doing a search on Jai's name. I couldn't quite believe the band was still together and performing, which was a ridiculous thing to think; it hadn't been that long since I'd last seen them play. But that world, Miriam's world, seemed at times so far away from me it felt like a dream.

I went to the show and the whole time Jai was playing I felt a lump in my throat. I went to the washroom before the performance ended. Luckily no one was in there, because I went into a stall and cried, like in that way where you have to hold your hand over your mouth to contain the sobs.

The sound a sarangi makes is an attempt to mimic the human voice, in particular the pain inherent in the human voice. This is what Jai told me back when he and Miriam were together and I shared with him that its sound stirred me so much, sometimes it made me want to weep. He explained that unlike any other instrument, the sarangi could produce almost all the nuances of vocal music. "The agony of being human," he said then, "is as complicated as it is beautiful."

By the time the performance ended, I'd pulled myself together. I waited outside the venue, a different one than where Miriam and I first met Jai. But as on that day he came out and chatted with people he seemed to know. It took him a while, maybe five or ten minutes, to see me. When he did, he smiled broadly and made his way to me quickly. We chatted briefly and agreed to meet the next day.

We sat on a bench under a tree. It was one of those extremely small parkettes that you find on busy streets in downtown Toronto, a sort of weak nod at keeping the city green. We had picked up coffees at a nearby café and decided to stop here because Jai didn't have a lot of time before he needed to return to his rehearsal. As soon as we were seated, I blurted that I was sorry. I asked him to forgive me for keeping him and Miriam apart. He looked startled.

"You didn't get back together because of me," I said. "Because of what I told you about her."

"You mean that time you phoned me?" he asked. "No," he said, waving his hand as though swatting away a small insect. "I knew that you were upset with your friend. I was upset with her too. I don't remember exactly, but I know I said terrible things about her during that call and, at other times, to her face. Much worse than anything you said."

As Jai was speaking, every once in a while he had to pause as a noisy car or motorcycle drove by. And when he did, he kept his eyes on me. But I looked away from him, at the passing vehicles or at the ground in front of me. I felt exposed in his presence and couldn't bear to look at him without a veil of words between us.

"I promise you what we talked about isn't the reason Miriam and I didn't get back together," he said. "I already knew all that about her. I knew, even if I was missing some details. We were finished before she started with Peter. Miriam and I were very different people. What we had wasn't going to last. I didn't want to face it because—it's as simple as this—we were married. You don't throw away a marriage. That's what I believed then. But what a stupid belief. Why not? If it's painful why not end it? After her affair I was so angry. I hated her for humiliating me. I couldn't understand how she could do that to me. But now, since she died, I have come to see she didn't know how to talk to a man. She couldn't find the words to say, this is what I want, or this is what I don't want, or I want to leave. She wanted to leave," Jai said. "In the end, then, she left."

After a short pause he added, "I have regrets too. She called me a few months before she died. She asked me to come see her. It was so difficult to do. I don't drive and where she was living then was not easy to reach. Also, I was busy and what would be the point? She only wanted help to get back with him. But if I had gone—" he said, cutting himself off. "Maybe I couldn't have saved her. But she might have given me the child."

He had been resting his elbows on his knees and was looking alternately at the ground and at me as he spoke, his coffee cup in his hands. "She had offered her to me once before."

I shook my head. "She wouldn't have left her daughter." I knew this. Without question, I knew this.

We sat in silence for a bit, watching the traffic. And then we talked about a few other things, about Dharm and the new vocalist, some grants he was applying for, that type of thing. Before parting, I asked him if he could give me the information about Miriam's and Zara's ashes. He had forgotten to do so years ago, or maybe I missed the email. I said the last part to be polite.

Again, he looked startled. "I must have misunderstood," he said. "I didn't realize I was meant to have sent you that information. I would not have forgotten."

"It's okay," I said. "I haven't had reason to travel to BC anyways. But I'll be going to Vancouver Island next month. I've rented a cabin and I'm hoping to do some writing. I'll finally have a chance to pay my respects to Miriam and Zara."

He told me the name of the cemetery and I wrote it down on the back of a notebook I had in my handbag. Then he promised to send me the location details of her columbarium. He had this information somewhere at home.

"I'm so pleased you came to the show yesterday," he said. "I've thought about you." He stopped and seemed to consider what he was going to say next. "It's good to see you."

"I can call you when I reach Victoria," I said, my voice trembling slightly.

He smiled. "I'll be waiting."

Miriam's and Zara's ashes were placed together in the same niche, he told me, on which was inscribed a quote from *The Waste Land* by T. S. Eliot. Peter told Jai that a slip of paper with a line from the poem—in Miriam's handwriting—was left on a desk in her house when she died. The house was tidy, everything put away. Peter deemed what was written on that piece of paper her final words. Jai remembered the name of the poem and the poet, but he couldn't remember the quote. He would send this to me later as well.

He didn't need to. I knew the words she had left behind.

"TIME AND SPACE are personal," Miriam was telling me. This was on an occasion before Zara, before Peter, before Jai. We were both students and living in Toronto, having brunch at that restaurant on College Street, the one that served home fries that tasted like ketchup chips. "Einstein, of course, used the term relativity because it's relative to us," she said, "but I prefer personal. Time and space are personal to me. And to you. They can stretch and dilate. They have to because the speed of light is constant."

"It's so weird," I said.

"It's math," Miriam said. "Calculations show us that it would take an infinite amount of energy for anything with mass to move at the speed of light. Which is an impossibility. And massless particles—photons—always travel at the speed of light. Nothing can move faster. So, imagine this, you are moving at half the speed of light and something comes toward you at three-quarters the speed of light. According to intuition, when it passes you, it should be going faster than the speed of light, right? But it doesn't. The speed of light remains constant. For you, in your personal experience, time will move slower to ensure the speed of light remains constant."

"Why?" I asked.

"The universe conspires to keep the speed of light constant," Miriam said.

"But why?"

"Okay," she said. "Listen. I'm going to explain something to you. The speed of light is special. It's not just a speed of something moving through space. As you move faster and faster and get closer to the speed of light, time slows down and space contracts." She leaned towards me.

"When you reach the speed of light, the entire universe becomes a single point, and time slows until it too becomes a point. Light doesn't experience space or time. The entire universe shifts around this constant, the speed of light."

I knew she would find this ridiculous. I knew she would dismiss me—probably irritably—but I had to ask. I had to say the words: "Do you think light is God? Not a personal God," I added quickly. "I know you don't believe in that; I don't either. But the power that made all of this," I said, waving my hand around to indicate the space around me, "that made everything?"

She smiled, a kind of placid smile. No laughing or eye rolling. No reminding me that here I go again—doctoral candidate in English literature—trying to jam science into metaphor, distorting it until it was nonsensical. "I remember so little of the day Salim died," she said. "The details have evaporated." Miriam had never talked to me about the day Salim died. She had told me details about the day before, when he drove off into the night. But she had not, until now, spoken about his final day on earth. "All that's left are fragments," she said.

"'These fragments I have shored against my ruins,'" I said.

"Yes," she whispered and then closed her eyes. "A nurse pursing her lips, her eyes welling with tears," she said. "A doctor, in a lab coat, bowing his head to give us the mercy of privacy. A lock of black hair having fallen on Salim's swollen forehead. It was Dad who sobbed, not Begum," she said, opening her eyes. "I think she was silent, at least at first. That can't be, can it? But this is the thing, the most amazing thing. I was looking at Salim; I wouldn't take my eyes off his face. I couldn't because how could switching off machines just switch him off too? Where would he go? And at some point, the doctor said he was gone. That's when Dad sobbed, and then, right then, I noticed that a beam of sunlight had come into the room and settled directly over Salim. On his face, his chest, and it stayed there, over him, enveloping him. I put my face next to his, my cheek on his cheek, and I could feel the warmth of the sunlight on me and in me. It filled me up. I was empty and it filled me up. I don't know how long it was, but at some point, Begum was losing it—screaming—and a nurse was helping me stand up and leading me out of the room. I turned back to look at him one more time before walking out and the sunlight was gone. He had changed. His face wasn't Salim anymore."

She was holding her hands over the table, palms facing up and hands open, as though she were about to catch someone who was falling.

"What was it?" she asked. "The light. Did it take him? Was he the light?"

Then she pressed her hands together, clasping them in front of her and leaning forward. "This is why I became a physicist, to enter the unknown, to go into it, deep into it. It doesn't scare me. It doesn't scare me, because I felt in those moments—in my being I felt it—that in this universe there is something. There's light and goodness. And it found him. It found us."

Epilogue

'M AT A cabin in Ucluelet, on Vancouver Island. It's small and has a faint, musty smell and no television or Wi-Fi. But my cellphone works well, and the owners left the kitchen fully stocked for me, which is a good thing because I haven't left the cabin since arriving more than a week ago. Jai is going to be here in a few hours. I called him yesterday. I had wanted to call him as soon as I arrived, but I couldn't. Miriam was demanding my attention. And I felt compelled to tell you everything about her, from our beginnings to her end. As I wrote, I imagined I was speaking to a kind, compassionate reader, someone who might forgive me despite everything I have done. Now that I've finished, I have come to realize I was only ever writing to myself.

Do you wonder, when you're talking to yourself, who is listening? Who is paying attention to the chatter and ruminating going on in your mind? Who or what is that quiet awareness? *Consciousness*, Miriam would answer. Consciousness, something her science couldn't fully explain but where, she taught me, reality comes into being.

Last night after I called Jai, I fell asleep to the sound of waves. I read somewhere that we are comforted by this sound because it is primal, an echo of the first sounds we heard as we came into being in our mother's womb: the gush of blood flowing powerfully—whoosh—out of her heart and—whoosh—back into her heart. The sound of life.

I slept peacefully the whole night. For the first time in years, Miriam didn't appear to me.

Acknowledgements

The lines in chapter 1 from the soundtrack of the Hindi film *Asli Naqli* are my own rendering. The lines in chapter 11 from "Ode to a Nightingale" are taken from *John Keats: The Oxford Authors* (Oxford University Press, 1990). The line by T. S. Eliot in chapter 23 is taken from *The Waste Land and Other Poems* (Broadview Press, 2010).

Portions of chapter 7 were previously published as a short story titled "Paper Crowns" in issue 156 (Fall 2020) of the *New Quarterly*.

I am grateful to the Ontario Arts Council and the Region of Waterloo Arts Fund for their financial support.

I offer my heartfelt thanks to the following people:

Habiba Jamal: for a lifetime of unconditional love and support.

Carrie Snyder and Emily Urquhart: for their friendship and wisdom; this book would not exist without the space we have created together.

Hilary McMahon at Westwood Creative Artists: for her infectious enthusiasm and support of my work.

Shivaun Hearne: for loving this book as much as I do, and for leading the wonderful team at House of Anansi who brought it to its final form.

Erin Bow and Stephanie Keating: for sharing their physics expertise; their input notwithstanding, any errors in expression of the science throughout these pages remain mine.

Wendy Stocker: for her meticulous proofreading.

Christian Snyder, Beth MacIntosh, and Dani Zaretsky: for granting me access to a room of my own, where I could work on the manuscript.

Craig Daniels: for everything.

TASNEEM JAMAL was born in Mbarara, Uganda, and immigrated to Canada in 1975. Her debut novel *Where the Air Is Sweet* was published to critical acclaim in 2014. That same year she was named one of 12 rising CanLit stars on CBC's annual list of Writers to Watch. Her writing has appeared in *Chatelaine, Saturday Night* magazine, and the *Literary Review of Canada*. She is the writing coach of The X Page Storytelling Workshop and an editor at the *New Quarterly* literary magazine. She lives in Kitchener.